W9-CZI-429

LENORE CURTIN had decided she would never love another man as long as she lived. Losing Walter had been too painful. Then Robert swept her off her feet, and her resolve weakened.

ROBERT DELANEY dazzled Lenore with his manly charm and take-charge attitude. But his possessive, demanding nature could also spell disaster.

CAROL LAMONTE wasn't satisfied sharing an office with Robert. She wanted Robert, and she was determined to win his heart at any cost!

Series Story Editor **Mary Ann Cooper** is America's foremost soap opera expert. She writes the nationally syndicated column *Speaking of Soaps*, is a major contributor to leading soap opera magazines, and is a radio and television personality.

Virginia Grace, author of *Forgive and Forget*, is an established writer who resides in Summit, New Jersey.

Dear Friend,

Publishing a paperback series such as the Soaps & Serials line can be very hard work indeed. Imagine reading thousands of scripts in search of exciting plots and characters! And that's just the beginning. Scores of writers and editors pool their talents to create a book that's authentic, dramatic and compelling.

Despite all our hard work at Pioneer Communications Network, Inc., we couldn't be a success without you, the reader. Since the first volumes of Soaps & Serials appeared in supermarkets and book stores across America, we have been overwhelmed by the enthusiastic reaction of readers. Many fans have graciously taken the time to write and tell us how much they enjoy Soaps & Serials.

Recently, a reader from South Bend, Indiana wrote: "These books are really neat! I've always loved watching ANOTHER WORLD, but now I'm more involved with the story than ever since I've been reading Soaps & Serials books." Many thanks to this reader and to all those who have supported our efforts to make our new genre of books a success.

For Soaps & Serials Books,

Mary Ann Cooper

Mary Ann Cooper

P.S. If you would like other volumes of Soaps & Serials books and can't find them in your local book source, see the order form inserted in the center of this book.

ANOTHER WORLD

6

FORGIVE AND FORGET

Soaps™ & Serials

PIONEER COMMUNICATIONS NETWORK, INC.

Forgive and Forget

ANOTHER WORLD paperback novels are published and distributed by Pioneer Communications Network, Inc.

SOAPS & SERIALS™ is a trademark of Pioneer Communications Network, Inc.

ISBN: 0-916217-36-1

Printed in Canada

10 9 8 7 6 5 4 3 2 1

FORGIVE AND FORGET

Chapter One
Winners and Losers

The former Mrs. Frame furiously paced back and forth across the linoleum kitchen floor, her heels clicking loudly with each step, her dark-chestnut hair snapping around at each turn.

"I'm a victim, that's what I am," she said. "You call that a divorce trial? You call that justice? I call it a conspiracy."

"Again? Let it go, Rachel," Ada said. She replaced the lid on the pot of homemade pea soup she had been stirring, then turned to face her gorgeous, irritable daughter. "Frankly, I'm sick of hearing about it. You come over here to the suburbs to visit maybe once every two months and you reward me with your pet peeves. You're a free, rich, attractive woman, Rachel. You've always been a survivor and you'll survive this—if your temper doesn't get you first. Oh, come on now. The divorce was over a month ago. It's final, it's legal, it's over."

Rachel narrowed her icy blue eyes. "I'm not letting Steve get away with it."

"Oh, are you telling me that your pride is hurt and you want revenge?"

"I—"

"Or are you saying you still love him?"

"That's a stupid question, Mother."

"Is it? How about an answer?"

"Steve's the father of my son."

"That's true. But you weren't married to Steve when you had Jamie, and you're not married to him now. Full circle. What could be more perfect? I'm sorry, I was kidding. Still, you have to face facts, Rachel, and stop acting like a spoiled brat. Now, get out the silverware and help me set the table."

Rachel felt anger rising within her. She wanted to lash out, scream, somehow force her mother to see her side. But the horrible truth was that Rachel wasn't sure what she felt. Rejection? Hurt? Rage? She yanked open the drawer. The silverware leaped and jingled like harsh chimes. She grabbed at knives and forks, squeezing each like a talisman to keep her cool.

Okay. All right. She had lost Steve, and it had taken a judge and a trial to do it, in front of all of Bay City, splashed across every society page: her marriage to the wealthy Steve Frame of Frame Enterprises, owner of just about everything and everybody, had been based on a fraud. In other words, the judge had decreed that Rachel had fraudulently coerced Steve to marry her.

Gee, Rachel thought, and wasn't it just dandy that her own father, Gerald Davis, had taken the stand against her. Yes, she decided, she'd lost more than a husband that day. Her pride, her heart, her very soul had been ripped out of her and put on public display. She knew that most people thought she deserved it.

She angled away from her mother, hiding a large

tear that suddenly rose from her eye. Yes, Rachel realized, what she was now feeling, and what she'd been feeling for the last terrible month, was humiliation.

So Rachel set the dining-room table in silence. She knew Ada was watching her with those sparkling, perceptive eyes. Protective Mom. Even though Ada was tough on Rachel, she had always been there, through Rachel's marriages and divorces, and Ada herself had gone through a divorce. Only from Ada, and no one else, could defensive, self-righteous Rachel bear to hear the stinging truth.

Soon the table was neatly set on a crisp white tablecloth, and Ada was dishing the feast into serving bowls and onto platters. Rachel, now calmed, moved to her mother's side and gave her a quick hug.

"You're a silly old woman, Ada," Rachel said.

"And you need me, don't you? Admit it."

"You're all I've got," Rachel said. She looked into her mother's round, kind face, at her matronly print dress, at her full figure and liked what she saw. Rachel lowered her cheek to her mother's shoulder.

Ada didn't know quite what to do. Not since Rachel had been a little girl had her daughter, the free spirit, the vixen, the scandalous talk-of-the-town, surrendered as she was doing now. Ada uneasily tried to comfort Rachel, half expecting Rachel to talk baby talk, half expecting her to snap and bite. When neither happened, and Ada was left just standing there feeling sorry but silly, she realized that, for now, Rachel was a defeated woman.

"Come on, kid," Ada said, "time to eat."

"I'm not hungry," Rachel said. She knew she sounded like a little girl, and for a moment it irritated her. "Is Gil home?"

"I heard him come in a few minutes ago. He'll be hungry, and that's for sure. Come on. Take out the ham."

Tall, mushy-looking, redheaded Gil McGowan, Ada's husband, was waiting for them in the dining room.

"You sick?" Gil said to Rachel. He moved to Ada and gave her two pecks on the cheek. She pecked him back, and he snuck in another peck as she was walking away.

"No, why?" Rachel said defensively.

"I don't know," Gil said. "I took a peek in the kitchen to see what smelled so good and saw you leaning on your mother. Thought you were sick or something, felt faint."

"I'm fine, just wonderful, never better," Rachel said.

Ada shook a finger at Gil. "I thought I told you not to wear your uniform at the table." Gil was a policeman.

"Oh," Gil said, looking at himself. "Habit, I guess."

Ada said, "When you wear your cop suit to the table I always think that if you don't like the meal I'll find myself in the slammer."

Gil smiled. "Don't worry. I'm off duty."

"Where's Jamie?" Rachel asked. Jamie, her son, the offspring of herself and Steve Frame when times between them had been more passionate and impulsive, lived with Ada and Gil.

"Oh, it slipped my mind," Ada said. "He's over at his friend's house—what's-his-name? Billy. He's eating over there tonight. He said he'll see you later if you can stay a bit after dinner."

Rachel nodded. She pursed her full red lips,

blinked and shrugged her shoulders. "It would have been good to see him."

Ada and Gil exchanged a look. Rachel had not to this point been a terribly needful mother. But now, the tone in Rachel's voice was one of needing, and it shocked Gil enough so his jaw dropped and Ada had to elbow him to close it.

"Come, let's eat," Ada said.

They sat down and began the meal. Food was what Rachel needed. It re-energized her. So she ranted and roared to Ada and Gil about the divorce. Soon Rachel and Gil were having their usual arguments, with Ada as referee, and the family was back to normal.

Ada was thoroughly enjoying herself, grateful for the private, warm moments with her wayward daughter earlier in the evening. She was proud of herself and thought that maybe she had even helped Rachel break her obsession for Steve Frame. Then, over dessert, out of the blue, Ada was brought back to reality.

"You know," Rachel said, swallowing a mouthful of chocolate cake, "I've got a feeling that I'm going to get one more shot at hotshot Steve Frame. In fact, I'm going to make a point of it."

The gleaming, steely Frame Enterprises Building towered over the business district of Bay City. From the penthouse window, the people looked ridiculously tiny, insignificant, yet Steve Frame knew that those tiny creatures were responsible for making him what he was. He looked down upon them with warmth.

Steve Frame narrowed his brown eyes and gazed past the city limits to the hills beyond. The rich, red September sunset had him mesmerized. Though he was a self-made millionaire, Steve knew that money wasn't the key to his success. From his poor beginnings to the present, money had always come to him, so easily that he took it for granted. No, Steve Frame was driven to create, to build buildings, to buy and organize football teams, stadiums, shipping lines, all multinational. Handsome, dynamic, Steve Frame was a powerful man with a heart and a conscience. He was both vulnerable and ruthless, sexual and intellectual, a man and a boy. He was a winner on a grand scale and often didn't realize it.

Steve refocused to the pane of glass before him. He saw his own clean-cut, well-built reflection, then he saw the expansive, masculine room behind him, then he saw long blond hair approaching from his left.

Alice took his arm and looked up into his strong face. "See any U.F.O.'s?"

Steve laughed, then melted when she gave him the full, wide smile he had first fallen in love with. "I see something more fantastic," he said. "I see the woman I'm going to marry next Saturday. I swear, I thought it would never happen."

They kissed deeply. He led her into the living room, across the thick white carpet, past the leather armchair and chrome-rimmed coffee table to the soft leather sofa. Alice slid the blanket of seal pelts over and they sat down upon it, getting comfortably close.

Alice held out her left hand and wiggled her fingers. They both admired her stunning diamond engagement ring. They kissed again. She looped her arm in his, settled her head on his firm chest, closed her eyes and sighed.

"It's really going to happen," she said. "I'm really marrying you. After everything, it is all going to work out."

"At last. Just as I knew it would," Steve said.

"Liar."

"What?"

"You thought we were doomed and you know it."

"Well, maybe a little doomed," Steve said.

"Definitely doomed."

"How doomed?"

Alice giggled. "Drastically, hysterically doomed."

They fell silent.

"It's not funny, is it?" Steve said.

"No," Alice said. "It is not that."

Steve had been married to Alice before, a lifetime ago, it now seemed. The shock of discovering that Steve had fathered Rachel's baby had driven Alice away, and when she had thought Rachel and he were having an affair, she had divorced him—a situation Rachel had orchestrated to devious perfection. And it was because of that child that Rachel had convinced Steve to marry her.

Alice had been in New York City then, as governess to Eliot and Iris Carrington's ill son, Dennis. Crushed over losing Steve, she had thrown all her energies and emotions into her work with Dennis. Meanwhile, in Bay City, Steve knew that his marriage to Rachel was a mistake. He still loved Alice desperately. And when Alice had returned with Eliot and Iris for Dennis's operation, she and Steve had been reunited and had quickly discovered they were still in love. They had also discovered that they had both been Rachel's pawns, and Steve had vowed to find a way to divorce Rachel.

Now, one month later, the ugly divorce trial was over, and Steve and Alice were free to chart their own futures. Alice thought it was nothing short of a miracle.

"They were betting against you at the trial, you know," Alice said.

Steve smiled. "I had a terrific lawyer. John couldn't have presented the case better."

Alice felt Steve grow tense. Something still bothered him about that trial. It was a tough thing to have gone through, Alice decided. After all, the great Steve Frame had been manipulated by a pretty face, and to drag all his dirty laundry out in public must have been very hard on him.

Alice rose from the sofa and moved around behind Steve. She began to knead Steve's neck and shoulders.

"Relax," she said. "Don't think about anything for a few minutes."

"This feels terrific."

"Shhh."

As her fingers worked their magic on his muscles, fear began once again to grip Alice's heart. Her world should be perfect now. She had Steve, security, the admiration and good wishes of almost everyone in Bay City. Yet she knew, because of her, Steve's world could never be perfect. How could she tell him? When? What would happen?

"Ow, not so hard, hon," Steve moaned.

"Sorry."

Poor Steve. The news she had to tell him was not good, and she suspected that she might not have the courage to tell him before they were married. After they were married it would be much worse, much more painful, but she couldn't bring herself to destroy their present idyll. Enjoy the good times while they are here. Worry about the future when it comes. Easier said than done.

Steve turned to face her. He immediately saw worry written all over Alice's lovely face. And as Alice had always done when things upset her, she began to fool with the ends of her straight blond hair.

"Troubles?" Steve asked. He took her hand. It was damp.

Alice shrugged. "Worried, I guess. About the wedding. The plans. You know."

"That it's all happening so quickly? Forget it. I know a lot of people, remember? And money talks. I've got half of Bay City working overtime. Everything will be ready by Saturday, don't you worry."

"I hope so."

"Know so. The new house is finished, just sitting there waiting for the new Mr. and Mrs. Frame. The honeymoon tickets are waiting at the airport. We're still young and the rest of our lives is ahead of us."

Alice managed a smile. The man was irresistible.

Steve rose, tossing a throw pillow back and forth between his hands like a football. "Let's have a bash. Dinner somewhere ridiculously expensive. What do you say?"

Alice shook her head. "I can't."

Steve playfully threw the pillow at her. She caught it and laughed.

"What do you mean you can't?" Steve said. "What, do you have a date or something?"

Alice nodded. "Yes, a very important date. I have the last fitting this evening for my wedding gown, remember?"

"Forget it," Steve said. "We'll be married naked."

Alice laughed wildly, throwing the pillow back to Steve, who allowed it to thump against his chest and fall to the floor.

"You're a wicked man, Steven Frame."

"I know," he said. He walked straight for her, up and over the sofa, and took her in his thick arms. "I'll miss you tonight. What are we doing tomorrow?"

"Don't you have a business to run?" Alice said through her laughter.

"Not this week, I'm too nervous. Too excited." He held her closer, enjoying the sweet aroma of shampoo on her hair. "We're a great pair, Alice. Great lovers, and we'll be great parents. I love you."

"I love you, too, Steve."

God, Alice thought, *I have to tell him. And I will. Soon.*

He helped her into her coat and walked her to the private elevator.

"Shall I have my driver take you to your fitting?" he asked.

She shook her head. "No, thanks. It's only a few blocks. I'll walk."

The phone rang.

"Business," Steve said. He kissed her quickly on the lips. "See you tomorrow, gorgeous."

"Okay."

Alice stepped into the elevator as Steve hurried over to answer the phone. When the elevator doors closed, Alice felt the tears coming. Steve's words continued to echo in her mind: *"We'll be great parents."*

You would be an excellent father, Steve, she thought. *You deserve it and I do love you. But I can never be a mother. It's medically impossible, Steve, you see . . . oh, why can't I tell him?*

Alice erupted with uncontrollable, lurching sobs.

* * *

For Alice, the week sped by on a wave of worry, elation, fear and love. The wildly contrasting emotions took their toll. When the wedding morning arrived, it was blessed with sunny, clear, warm weather, and Alice was a nervous wreck and drawn.

"The new-bride blues," said one of Alice's young bride's maids, as she fussed about Alice in the grand dressing room in the east wing of Steve's—their —new mansion. "A little rouge here, highlight there and you'll be good as new."

Downstairs, she knew, the guests were arriving. Minutes now, minutes away from being Mrs. Steven Frame. Minutes away from marrying the man she loved without telling him that she was unable to give him the children he so desperately desired. And, perhaps, mere hours away from rejection and divorce.

The music began. There was no more time for tears. Too late for truth. She'd have to hope and pray Steve loved her enough to understand and settle for less than a wife and a mother.

Alice rose and was soon descending the grand staircase that emptied into the morning room, where the ceremony was to take place. She saw hundreds of flowers, familiar faces, golden sunbeams stretching across the room. And there, in the middle of all of it, like an Adonis at the gates to paradise, was her handsome Steve.

The next conscious thought Alice had was that it was all over. Her veil was up and Steve was kissing her. Organ music throbbed in her ears, people were whispering their congratulations. She looked up into Steve's face and there was a tear on the lid of his left eye. She hugged him desperately and felt a surge of confidence that flooded her with warmth. Suddenly it was the happiest day of her life.

The next few hours were a whirl of partying on the outside patio. The band was superb and lively, the guests were joyous and Alice flitted from one to the other, then immediately back to Steve. She couldn't bring herself to leave his side for long.

Then, suddenly, Steve wasn't there. Five minutes, ten, twenty. Where had he gone? Alice searched, and eventually found Steve in the study on the main floor. He was seated, bent over at the waist in a leather chair. Before him stood two men she did not recognize.

"Is anything wrong?" she asked.

The taller of the two men looked at her sadly. "We thought it best to wait at least until after the wedding."

Alice panicked. "Steve, what is it? Tell me." She clutched the skirts of her wedding dress.

Steve rose and came to her, then he turned back to the men. "Give us a few minutes, will you?"

The men nodded and left.

"Steve?"

Steve swallowed hard. "Those men are from the district attorney's office, Alice. It seems I am under arrest. But don't worry—"

"Arrest! Why? What do they say you've done?"

"It's not what they say I've done, darling. It is what I have done. At my trial, my divorce from Rachel, I was desperate, to say the least. I didn't think I had a chance of getting out of the marriage. So I did a stupid thing."

Steve fell silent for a moment, and in that silence

Alice saw the future slipping away. "Tell me, Steve, please."

Steve stroked her face before he spoke. "You know Gerald Davis, Rachel's father? Of course you do. He's a desperate man, big money problems. And he and Rachel, to say the least, never got along. Anyway, I saw an opportunity. Like I said, I was desperate and—"

"What, Steve?"

"I bribed him to lie in court. He agreed. He substantiated my claim of fraud. This doesn't affect the divorce or anything, it still stands. But Alice, darling, on this our happiest day, I have been arrested for bribery and perjury."

"Oh, God," Alice said. She slumped into the chair. "What are you going to do? What's going to happen? Why did Gerald turn on you?"

"He didn't. John did."

"What? John Randolph?"

Steve nodded. "My lawyer, my trusted friend. He discovered what I'd done and told the authorities. I'll never forgive him for this. *Never!*"

"Steve, I'm scared."

Steve knelt beside her and cradled her head against his shoulder. "Don't worry. It'll all turn out right. You'll see. Those men want me to go downtown for a while. I'll be back in no time, you'll see."

Alice felt herself slipping into shock, unable to speak, unable to feel or react.

Two weeks later, Steve was sentenced to six months in prison. Before they took him away, they allowed him to say good-bye to Alice.

Suffering and guilt had tightened Steve's face. "Don't cry, hon," he said. "It'll all be over soon. I'll pay for what I've done and it'll be over. Our lives are before us—love, home, security and kids, lots of kids."

Alice tore away from his arms and ran out of the courthouse. After all that had happened, she knew she could never tell him the truth. She could never face him again.

"I'm an honest man, I am," John Randolph said to the bartender.

"I know you are, Mr. Randolph."

"Gimme another. Nearly two months ago my whole life fell apart. Did I tell you that?"

"No, sir."

"Well, it did. I've got a big house, cars, a mansion with plenty of imported stuff inside. But just like that, I lost my law business, crumbled at my feet. I used to work for Steve Frame, handled all his legal work, did good, too. Fired me. Just before he went to prison. Canned me for being an honest man. Was in all the papers. The crook."

"Think maybe it's time to be heading home, Mr. Randolph?"

John shook his head. "Can't take Pat anymore. She hates me for, as she says, 'betraying Steve.' I'm a betrayer now. Before, I was an ethical and successful lawyer. Now I'm Judas. Now I'm also a drinker. Never was before. Am now. Life, my good friend, is very cruel, indeed."

And John Randolph, formerly one of the most powerful attorneys in the Bay City area, lowered his head to his folded arms and wept.

Chapter Two
Chances

October was Lenore Curtin's favorite time of year. After the hot and before the cold. It energized her, filled her with a spunk she rarely felt. She tooled her station wagon up the long drive to the large Victorian home she had fallen in love with at first sight. Lenore loved things of quality.

"Hurry up now, Wally. Get the groceries inside before the ice cream melts."

"Okay, Mom!"

She watched lovingly in the rear-view mirror as little Wally burst out of the car and ran to the rear, threw open the hatch and struggled to lift one of the heavier bags. He checked to see if she was watching, then quickly grabbed a smaller bag and zigzagged his way toward the front door.

Lenore's eyes moved to her own reflection. Getting older, definitely, but still beautifully plain. She stuck her tongue out at herself and began bringing in the rest of the bags.

The truth was that Lenore was a gorgeous woman who didn't know it. Her thick, flowing sandy hair and deep-blue eyes always drew the attention of men. But Lenore wasn't shopping for men and never noticed. People said she was the most impossibly eligible single woman in Bay City.

With all the groceries in the newly renovated kitchen—Lenore had finally opened her checkbook and bought all the luxury appliances she'd ever wanted—Wally began climbing on the counters to put items away.

"Don't stand up there!" Lenore shrieked. "You're going to scare me to death, you monkey."

She walked over to where Wally was giggling on the counter and reached out for him. He hugged her with arms and legs and rode her around as Lenore spun in circles, peppering him with kisses. Then she put him down, instructing him that it was his job to put away groceries on the lower level. Wally liked that job and immediately crawled under the sink.

Her son was the world to Lenore. In fact, he was all she had since Walter had died. The thought made her shudder. She looked back at her small boy. If Wally ever found out the truth about his father, it would ruin him for life. Never, she vowed again, never will Wally discover that his father was a . . . the word came hard . . . a murderer. She tried to put the thought out of her mind but, for the millionth time, the scenes from the past flickered before her mind's eye.

Walter, her husband, once a respected district attorney. Walter, greedy, quitting his D.A. job to become a partner in John Randolph's law firm. Walter, jealous, willing to believe the worst about her. Walter, desperate, falling in with shifty Wayne Addison.

Wayne, to rid himself of the persistent Liz Matthews, had lied and told Liz he was having an affair with Lenore behind Walter's back. Soon after, Wayne's body was found, murdered.

No one knew who had committed the crime. Until witnesses said they had seen Lenore leave Wayne's apartment on the night of his death. Lenore had tried to explain she had only been returning some documents, but with the help of the vindictive Liz, Lenore had been indicted for murder.

Walter had defended her and gotten her acquitted. Then, some time later, Walter had dropped the horrible bombshell. He had confessed to Lenore that he'd found out that Wayne was having an affair with her. He had gone crazy and killed Wayne. Walter had said that he couldn't stand living with his guilt anymore, and he'd drive over to tell the authorities. Walter never returned. His body was found in his mangled car.

The trauma of discovering that the man she had been married to, the man she had loved and trusted, had committed murder and then allowed her to stand trial, crushed Lenore. That was the tragic truth Lenore was living with, the truth that had thrown her into self-imposed exile from all men and the truth she had to protect Wally from at all costs.

"Come here, you little brat," Lenore said to Wally.

Wally ran into her arms. She hugged him tightly. "What do you want for dinner?"

"Pizza!"

"You got it."

Lenore got busy making dinner, not telling Wally he'd be eating a healthy salad before he ate his pizza.

Her mind moved to the next day at work. She held a good position at Frame Enterprises; she had a job she liked and was very good at. But what she was thinking about now was the scandal. Rumors flew up and down the halls every day about how the long arm of the law had reached out and grabbed Bay City's most prosperous young tycoon on his wedding day and slapped him into jail. It was the stuff of novels and endless gossip. No one, Lenore knew, cared about the facts. They wanted to juice it up, and juice it up they did.

The gabby gossips speculated in whispered tones that Steve's jailing was all set up as a power move by Steve's younger brother, Willis Frame. Then they switched theories and said Steve had arranged the whole thing, to put himself in prison and away from dangerous men who were out to get him. And often, far too often, people would state that Rachel was behind the whole thing, the humiliated ex-wife, the spitfire who never lost a man unless she herself rejected him. If Rachel couldn't have Steve, then no one could have him. Let him rot in prison.

Lenore shook her head as she spread the sauce on the pizza dough. "Fools," she said.

The television was blaring in the other room, and Wally burst into gunfire giggles.

Lenore shook her head again, happy with her life as it was, grateful for what she had, content with who she was. *I've got all I want*, she thought. *And the only thing I'd ever want to get rid of are the memories, the horrible memories.*

The next day, with Wally off to school, Lenore arrived at work early. It was convention time, and Frame Enterprises was humming. As an interdepartmental coordinator, Lenore was extremely busy.

At 9:05, the mail was dropped off in Lenore's office by a rotund and comical mail-room employee.

"Hey, Miss Curtin," he said, "have you heard the latest?"

"What?" Lenore said, shuffling through papers, irritated and curious at the same time.

"Mr. Frame's planning a prison break. Honest. Haven't heard exactly when, but the girl in the cafeteria told me—"

Lenore laughed. "Will you get the heck out of here!"

He smiled and waddled out of her office.

Lenore immersed herself in her work, and the morning whizzed by. Just before lunch, Janet Williams, an executive with Frame Construction and one of Lenore's few friends, came into her office, closed the door and sat down.

"So?" Janet said, primping her curly black hair. "Are you going?"

"To what?" Lenore said.

"To what, she asks. As if she didn't know. The party, tomorrow night. You sent the memo yourself, remember? Builders, construction people, architects, planners."

"Oh, that party," Lenore said, still busy with paperwork. "No, I'm not going."

"Why not?"

Lenore laid down her pencil. "Why not? I'm busy, that's why not. I'm working at home these nights, and there's Wally to consider. I'm sure the party will be terrific without me."

Janet sighed. "I'm worried about you, Lennie."

"Stop worrying. I'm fine."

"You're not fine. You're lonely. You need to get out. Besides, you've been with Frame Enterprises a long time. You're bright, know the business. It's time for you to branch out, advance your career, make new opportunities, contacts. The people at this party are exactly the people you should be rubbing elbows with."

Lenore looked up at skinny Janet with a wry smile. "You mean you think I should meet some men, have some flings, kick off my shoes."

"Who knows what's going to happen? There's a whole world out there, Lennie. What do you say? You can come with me, we'll be a team."

"Sorry, but no. Thanks for thinking of me, though."

"Know what? I think you're afraid."

"Janet, trust me. I'm not afraid. I'm simply too busy."

"Contacts. Opportunities. More money. Not to mention men. Think about it."

"I have."

"Think again."

Lenore checked her watch. "I'm late! Sorry, Janet, I've got a luncheon meeting. Thanks for the thought. See you later."

As Lenore rushed down the hall, Janet called after her, "Meet me at eight tomorrow night?"

Lenore stopped and turned. "No!"

The next evening after dinner, Wally was with a baby-sitter and Lenore was searching through her wardrobe for the perfect party dress. It had to be both festive and businesslike. Slightly sexy and conservative at the same time.

"Janet, if this turns out to be a fiasco I'll never forgive you. Ah!"

Lenore pulled from her closet a deep-blue dress of

heavy silk. The perfect thing. As she dressed, she couldn't help feeling as if she were going to a prom instead of a business party. She couldn't help fixing each long, sandy lock and each stroke of eyeliner to perfection. She couldn't help fantasizing walking into the room and watching every male jaw in the place drop wide open.

Despite her stubbornness, Lenore was looking forward to the party. She was also afraid.

Janet, in her usual flamboyant style, had hired a driver for the evening. The long Lincoln pulled up in front of Lenore's house at 7:50 P.M. It was cool and raining, and the driver met Lenore at the front door with a huge umbrella. He escorted her to the rear door and Lenore slid inside.

"Well, good evening, Cinderella," Janet said.

"Hi," Lenore said.

Beneath her thin peach-colored raincoat, Janet was wearing a shocking-red party dress with a deep V neckline, which drew attention to Janet's only major bodily assets. Lenore knew, right then, that Janet was not going to the party for business. She was going to get down to business with men. Beside her, Lenore felt plain but secure. Maybe Janet would get all the attention and the wolves would leave her alone.

They checked their coats in the lobby and together walked into the Sunset Room of the High Court Hotel. The room was filled with well-dressed people, chatting comfortably. So far, Lenore was not sorry she had come.

Done in various tasteful tones of red, purple, orange and yellow, the Sunset Room virtually dragged Lenore into its warmth. Dotted around the parqueted dance floor were the tables, each with a vase of flowers. At the far end was the banquet buffet, with lavish arrangements of meats, seafood, fruits, salads, breads and cheeses. To the side of that was the bar. And at the other end of the room the orchestra was playing a jazzed-up version of "When I'm Sixty-Four." It was a twenty-piece ensemble of violins, cellos, brass, electric guitars and drums. A male and a female singer stood center stage, taking turns singing earnestly into their cordless microphones.

A bald man in a black tuxedo approached them. "Excuse me. Names, please."

The two women gave their names, and the bald man wrote them on respective name stickers.

"If you don't wear the name, you can't play the game," the man said.

Janet was clearly irritated. "That doesn't make any sense and you know it. Do we have to wear these things?"

"Absolutely," the bald man said. "Look around you. Presidents, vice-presidents, executive counsels. If they can wear them, surely you two fillies can."

The bald man made a mock gesture of sticking Janet's name badge on for her. His aim was lecherously low.

Janet grabbed his wrist and plucked the sticker from his fingers. Then she gestured to Lenore. "May I introduce you, you jerk, to Lenore Curtin. President of Curtin International."

"Oh," the bald man said, flushing deeply, blinking, stammering. "I . . . I didn't know. My apologies, no insults meant."

Janet went on. "Lenore works for me. Not bad for two fillies, wouldn't you say? Now, run off and mop the floors or something, will you?"

Without another word, the bald man vanished. Janet and Lenore burst into gales of laughter.

"I don't believe you did that!" Lenore said.

"I hate creeps like that," Janet said. "Come on, let's mingle."

Lenore was now not only glad she had come, but glad she was with Janet. She felt protected and safe. So with Janet at her side, Lenore, untouched glass of champagne in her hand, made the rounds. She was astonished at how many people Janet knew. And Lenore was meeting them all, some nice, some otherwise. Lenore was asked to dance a number of times, but politely refused, opting to stand and watch Janet perform.

Lenore had vague hopes of making some contacts here, the seed planted by Janet. But as things were turning out, there just was no opportunity. This was a social gathering, a chat-fest, a release from previous days of meetings and meetings to come. This left Lenore without a purpose, and though she was truly enjoying watching others enjoy themselves, she felt distinctly uncomfortable.

An hour later, Janet had disappeared on the arm of a tall, good-looking man in a Texan hat. Alone now, Lenore began to think about going home, picking up Wally and perhaps spending the rest of the rainy evening playing a game.

But it was not to be.

Toward her, with a wide smile on his handsome face, came a well-built man with dark, wavy hair. Yes, he was definitely heading right for Lenore. He was still too far away for her to read his name badge. And when she could, he was already upon her, extending his hand and introducing himself.

"Excuse me, my name is Robert Delaney," he said with a resonant voice.

Lenore shook his hand firmly. "Hello."

He bent to read her badge. "Lenore Curtin, yes. Nice to meet you, Lenore. I was talking with Janet Williams a moment ago and she said you might be interested in a little talk."

Oh, no, Lenore thought. Had Janet told him she was president of Curtin International? She almost giggled at the thought.

"What kind of talk?"

Robert turned and took a look around him. "I don't believe this crowd, do you? I do business with half of them, but I've never seen them act like schoolchildren before." He turned back to Lenore. "It's nice to finally meet someone who's willing to talk seriously, even for a moment. So, answering your question, Janet mentioned that a little talk might do you a world of good."

That was a strange way to put things, but Lenore liked this man's demeanor, his direct and honest approach. She relaxed. "Well, Mr. Delaney—"

"Come on. Robert."

"Thank you. But Janet isn't any more sure of what I want than I am. I guess I just want to learn more about what's out there in the real business world."

"Remind me, whom do you work for now?"

"Frame Enterprises."

"That's right. Janet told me and I clear forgot."

"What business are you in?" Lenore asked.

"My own. I run my own architectural outfit. Doing fairly well. Been in business six years and nothing's fallen down yet."

Lenore laughed.

"Hungry or anything, Lenore?"

"I wouldn't mind trading in this champagne for a Perrier."

"Even better, why don't we take a table and indulge in the feast? The food is much better than the champagne, I assure you. This way."

Before Lenore could tell him she wasn't actually hungry, he led her by the elbow to a table, excused himself, then returned with two plates of food and two glasses of punch.

"Now, that's more like it, isn't it?" Robert said.

"Thank you."

They began to eat.

He touched her upper arm. "Let me tell you something, Lenore. Being an architect is fascinating. No other big business allows you the freedom of direct creation. If you're interested in expressing yourself, take a look in. In fact, I insist you come over to my offices and I'll give you a grand tour."

Only after Robert had finished speaking did Lenore finally realize he had touched her arm. She had accepted it naturally—not that it was a big event or anything, but it did mean something, somehow.

"I'd like that," Lenore said.

Their eyes locked for a moment, and Lenore relaxed even more.

"So tell me about yourself," he said. "Give me your whole history, your life story."

"Well," Lenore said, swallowing, "I've been at Frame nearly six years. Climbed up the ladder of success from secretary. The last two years I've been moving kind of sideways."

"Married?"

"No, my husband . . ." She paused for only a fraction of a second, but many thoughts went through her mind. His personal question was sudden, took her by surprise, and she found herself answering. Should she? It seemed natural. In fact, she already trusted him and on one level wanted him to know. She felt he cared, and she hadn't really talked with anyone so long. "My husband is deceased. I have a little boy named Wally, and I live in a wonderful old house about three miles from here."

"I see," he said. "I'm sorry. Janet tells me you don't get out too much."

That loudmouth! Janet really had gone too far. Lenore wondered how she could get out of this one. She countered, "Do you?"

Robert smiled. "Touchy area? Fine. I'm sorry. How about if I confess? I'm not married either and I don't get out much. I'm obsessed with my work, I'm selfish and protective of my time. My new offices are only a block from Frame—my building is quite a bit smaller, but since I'm the one who designed it, it's much more impressive—and I live out in the sticks in a home preposterously built into the side of a cliff. Come on, let's dance."

Lenore barely had time to wipe her lips with the napkin. Robert whisked her off to the dance floor. The orchestra was playing "Blue Moon." Robert confidently took her in his arms and skillfully maneuvered her through the crowd of dancing couples.

What a marvelous dancer, she thought. He moved smoothly, without suddenness. He held her close, but not too close. Lenore felt her heart shamelessly picking up speed.

They danced the next number, then sat the following two out. Their conversation was unrushed yet exciting. Lenore discovered that they had a lot in common, and they discussed and compared interests right down to favorite colors. A few times Lenore felt like a schoolgirl, but the feeling was good. She laughed. He laughed. Without a word, they rose to dance again.

This time he held her closer, and Lenore did not resist. He said quietly into her ear, "You know, Lenore, I think Janet was trying to play Cupid with us."

"Oh?"

"Definitely."

"I don't doubt it. Have you known her long?"

"Never met her in my life," Robert said.

"What!" Lenore pulled back from him a little to get a good look at his face. He was smiling widely. "But you said she sent you over."

Robert shrugged. "I lied. I saw you walk in with her. It was easy enough to sneak a look at her name badge. I had to think of some way of meeting you."

Lenore didn't know whether to be angry or ecstatic. She searched his face for more signs of deviousness, but saw none.

"What else was a lie?" Lenore said.

"Nothing, I swear. But I had to confess that one little thing."

"One little thing," Lenore repeated with a low laugh. "You've really never met Janet?"

"Couldn't even remember her now to pick her out of the crowd."

Robert began to laugh. And when Lenore broke

into a smile, he laughed harder and she joined him. The band struck up a fast number, and Lenore danced like she hadn't danced for years.

"Whew!" Lenore said, fanning herself with her hand. "I've got to sit down."

Robert sat down beside her. "I'm too old for this."

"What? You're not much older than I am."

"Whoops. In that case, I take it back."

Lenore laughed. She checked her watch. "Time to go," she said. "Have to pick up Wally from the baby-sitter."

"Let me walk you to the door."

On the way to the lobby, Lenore wondered how she would get home. She hadn't seen Janet for hours. Had she left? Lenore's pulse quickened. Though she had enjoyed the evening and liked Robert very much, she wasn't ready to drive off with him—with him or anyone else. Lenore considered the evening over, and she took it for granted that she would not see Robert Delaney again. Since Walter's death and the awful truth she'd learned about him, Lenore had not opened up her heart to anyone. And she was not prepared to begin now.

The man in the coatroom presented Lenore with her coat, then handed her a note. It was from Janet, saying that she had gone but the hired car was all Lenore's. Great relief washed over Lenore.

She turned to Robert. "Thank you for a wonderful time. I'm really glad you were here, and your little deception was very flattering."

"You're welcome," Robert said, helping her into her coat. "How about that invitation to come over to my offices?"

"I'll think about it," Lenore said, now anxious to

leave. She held out her hand. "Again, thanks, Robert."

He took her hand but instead of shaking it firmly, he held it softly for a moment, gave it a small squeeze, then let it go.

"Good night," he said. His smile was sorrowful, his brown eyes pools of sincerity.

Lenore awkwardly swooshed her sandy hair behind her with the back of her hand. "Good night."

It was still raining, though not as hard. The doorman soon had Lenore's car out front, and she hopped in. She gave the driver directions to Wally's baby-sitter, then sat back with a huge, satisfied sigh.

It had been a good evening. He was good company. And, she was stunned to admit to herself, she missed him already. But chances were something Lenore hadn't taken in a long while. No, she thought, keep life simple, easy. She thought about Wally.

Two evenings later, the phone rang in Lenore's house. She answered. It was Robert. There was a new Broadway musical making a tour through town. Would she care to join him?

Without hesitation, Lenore said a confident yes.

Chapter Three
Healing and Hoping

Millionaire Mackenzie "Mac" Cory had returned from New York City to his Bay City mansion three weeks ago, mid-February, and it felt good to be back. He loved Bay City: its ever-changing business community, its controversial politics, its lively social life and its lovely women. For a Midwestern town, it really hopped. And at a healthy, handsome fifty-seven years of age, Mac was prepared to take it on. But first there were serious matters to attend to.

This bright and sunny March morning, Mac was worried. He had risen at 5:00 A.M. and was now pacing the floor of his massive bedroom in his silk pajamas. He'd called the hospital four times already, but no one had returned his calls.

Someone knocked on his bedroom door.

"Come in," Mac said.

Opening the door was his tall head butler, Simon. Perched at an absolute level on Simon's wide, experienced hand was a silver tray with breakfast.

"I didn't ask for that," Mac said grumpily.

"Sir, I know you well enough by now."

"Yes, you do, Simon. Yes, you certainly do. And let me tell you that it irritates me from time to time."

"Yes, sir."

Simon set the tray down on the table by the bay window. Simon turned to go.

"Simon?" Mac said.

"Sir?"

"Thanks a lot."

"You're welcome, sir."

Simon left.

The toast, coffee, eggs and sweet rolls did Mac a measure of good. He was now energized, and if the hospital wasn't going to call him back, he'd just get down there himself to see what was happening.

He moved toward his closet.

The phone rang, his private line. He yanked the receiver off the cradle and brought it to his ear. "Yes? Yes?"

"Mac Cory?" the voice on the other end said.

"Russ, that you?"

"Yes. Sorry I didn't get back to you sooner, but I've been busy."

"Well, what's the news?" Mac walked to the window and stared out across the gardens and his thirty acres of prime real estate.

"Dennis is fine, everything went okay," Russ said. "He's been in the recovery room a little over two hours now and should be out pretty much the rest of the day. We'll know more once he wakes up and starts eating, but it is my opinion that the surgery went excellently. I have every hope of complete recovery."

"God, that's good news," Mac said. "Thank you, Russ. You're a mighty fine doctor. Have you told Iris and Eliot yet?"

"I was going to call them as soon as I hung up with you."

"Well, hang up already," Mac said. "And thanks."

Mac replaced the phone and sighed heavily. Good news—nothing in this world beats good news about someone you love.

Dennis Carrington was Mac's grandson, a boy who had spent most of his ten years in and out of hospitals. And when Dennis wasn't in a hospital, he had to be taken care of at home. That was Alice's job, a job everyone in the family loved her for. Everyone, that is, except Iris—Mac's daughter, Dennis's mother, Eliot Carrington's recent ex-wife.

"What a family," Mac said, shaking his head as his valet helped him dress.

The first reason Mac had returned to Bay City was Dennis's all-important heart operation at the skilled hands of Russ Matthews. The second reason he'd returned was his daughter, Iris.

Iris had never had it easy but, as Mac well knew, ninety-nine percent of Iris's troubles were because of Iris. As a wife to the successful writer Eliot Carrington in New York City, she'd been a fire storm—jealous, nagging, possessive. Mac could never figure out what had drawn those two together, but that was all water under the bridge now, for Iris's emotions had exploded on her.

With Dennis getting sicker every day, Iris had tried to help so insistently that she actually became the bigger problem. Dennis turned off to her, and she upset him every time she entered his room. Not knowing what to do with all her emotional energy, she turned elsewhere.

Thus began a tangled web that Mac had to think hard about to sort out. Alice had been living in Iris's and Eliot's home as governess, and Iris became insanely jealous. She suspected Alice and Eliot of carrying on behind her back, even though, at the time, Alice was still married to Steve Frame. And when Eliot and Alice had to take Dennis to Saint Croix, Iris called Rachel, explained things and got Rachel to take Steve there and "accidentally" bump into Eliot and Alice.

Iris had hoped that Steve would think Eliot and Alice were having an affair, and that Steve would drag Alice back to Bay City by her hair, and clean out of Iris's life. That didn't happen. Rachel had done her work far too well. What happened was that both Steve and Alice thought the other was having an affair, and the whole event sparked what was to be Alice's divorce from Steve.

So there was poor, deceitful Iris with her life around her knees. Not only did Alice stay, but she and Eliot became even closer friends. But the worst thing of all was that Alice seemed closer to Iris's son than Iris herself was.

In short, Iris had a severe nervous breakdown. She couldn't cope with her suspicions and deadly imagination. She divorced Eliot and returned to Bay City. Soon everyone else returned to Bay City for Dennis's operation, and Iris was suddenly near the family but out of it at the same time.

Now Iris was getting better. She had hopes of

renewing her relationship with her son. But she needed help. Enter Mac.

"Tell me something, David," Mac said to his valet, "how long have you been with me?"

"Fourteen years, sir."

"Have you ever seen such a screwed-up family?"

"I really couldn't say, sir. Yours is the only one I've ever worked for."

"Wisely diplomatic, David. That'll be all. Thanks."

David exited.

Simon entered.

"Your daughter, Iris, is downstairs, sir."

Mac checked his watch. "Fifteen minutes since she received Russ's call. Wonder what took her so long. I'm right behind you, Simon."

Iris wanted to hug her father when he walked into the grand living room. She was bursting with joy at the good news about Dennis's successful surgery. But she and her father had never had a hugging relationship, so instead she gave him a polite kiss on the cheek.

"Isn't it the best news in the world?" Iris said to Mac.

"It certainly is. What we've been waiting for. How are you doing?"

"Fine, fine."

Mac thought Iris looked just about as she always had. Bleached blond hair to her shoulders, all done up complicatedly. Pinched, red-lipped smile. Piercing, jittery brown eyes. And her conservative clothes perpetually contrasted with her frantic, grasping personality. But even at that, especially considering Iris's good figure, she was an attractive young woman.

"You look skinny," Mac said.

"I'm fine, Mac, honest," Iris said. She had always called her father by his first name. Never Dad or Daddy, or even Father. This in itself reminded Iris of her distance from her father.

"Maybe it's the dress you're wearing," Mac said. "You look all stiff, dark, like you're in mourning or something."

"Always criticizing."

"On the contrary," Mac said. "Always helpful. Depends how you want to look at it."

Iris stomped her foot. "Can't you be nice for a change?"

"I'm always nice, honey," Mac said. "You just expect too much."

Iris fell silent. She knew what he said was true. She did expect too much, especially where Mac was concerned. She had been raised in Swiss boarding schools, away from house and home, away from her father, growing up with people who inevitably became strangers. She and her father simply never had a chance. But now, more than ever before, husband-less, emotionally unstable Iris needed her father's love. Love that had eluded her all her life. Love that she had recently discovered she missed very much. She felt it was no little coincidence that Mac was now back in Bay City. This was her chance to have the father she had never had, and she wanted to do everything in her power to help him see her through new eyes. Even if it meant she had to change.

"Let's go out and have us a really nice breakfast," Iris said. "What do you say?"

Mac checked his watch. "Ten-thirty. Just had a little breakfast about seven o'clock."

How can he be so insensitive? Iris wondered. *Doesn't he realize this is a good chance to have a little time with his daughter? Doesn't he want to?*

"All right, then," Iris said. "We'll have brunch. Dennis won't be able to have visitors until later in the day. We can take our time, work up a good hunger."

Mac shot her with his finger. "You're on."

Mac called for his driver, and in ten minutes they were on their way.

Alice had been at the hospital since three o'clock in the morning. At seven-thirty, after he had made all his phone calls, Russ Matthews came down and told Alice the good news about Dennis. Then Russ took her up to his office because Alice looked worse than he had ever seen her.

Russ's office was large, a corner office with three large windows on the fifth floor of the hospital. Alice could barely walk on her own, and he helped her onto the large leather sofa. He propped a pillow under her head.

"I'm a wreck, aren't I?" Alice said.

"Not too bad," Russ lied.

Alice looked up into his kind, big-boned face. "I'm sorry I keep coming back here. The last few months haven't been easy."

"I know," Russ said. "Well, at least we don't have to worry about Dennis for now."

"I'm so glad," Alice said weakly.

"Have you eaten?"

When Alice didn't answer, Russ picked up the phone and ordered her some breakfast. Then he pulled a chair over by the sofa and sat down beside her.

Alice quietly began to weep.

"No better?" Russ asked.

Alice shook her head and turned her face away from Russ.

For the last few months, ever since Steve's imprisonment, Alice had come to Russ for help from time to time. And each time Russ had seen her, she had gotten worse. Depression, fear, general lack of focus and loss of hope. Russ suggested a psychiatrist, but Alice firmly refused. Russ understood, because the foundation on which Alice had built her emotional turmoil was shame. Only to someone she knew and trusted could she tell her deepest fears. And Russ knew he was the only one she had opened up to.

"I . . . I keep going over and over it in my mind," Alice said, accepting the Kleenex Russ offered. "I keep picturing myself meeting Steve when he's released and telling him the truth. But each time, the picture goes black. It won't work, Russ. I can't do it. I've lied to him, deceived him, betrayed him. How can I tell him something like this after he's suffered months in prison? It would crush him."

"He might understand," Russ said. "He loves you, you know."

"Love only makes up for so much sin."

"Alice, you haven't sinned. The problem you have has nothing to do with you, with your self-worth, with your goodness. Your problem is strictly physical. Many, many women out there are unable to bear children, and they are leading happy, loving married lives."

Alice sobbed harder, almost uncontrollably. "I . . . I should have told him. He'll hate me. I . . . I just can't bear to face him, Russ. I won't!"

"Listen to me, Alice—"

"No more talk!" she screamed, then clamped a

hand over her mouth and settled back into the sofa. "I'm sorry. But I just had word that Steve is getting out of prison early."

"Really?" Russ said, then was afraid to ask: "When?"

Alice's eyes grew wide, and she looked fearfully through her tears at Russ. "Tomorrow. Oh, God, tomorrow."

Russ considered again, as he had in the past, giving Alice a drug to calm her down. But he had known her a very long time, and he felt that she could conquer this depression. He was sure that deep inside her was strength. He'd seen the strength in her before, and if he could just say the right words, get her believing in herself, he was fairly sure he could pull that strength to the surface.

A candy striper knocked on the door, then entered with Alice's breakfast. Russ thanked her and she left. Alice sat up and ate eagerly.

"Oh, boy, that was good," Alice said. "Thank you."

Russ noticed that a bit of healthy color had come back into her cheeks, and he wondered just how long it had been since she'd last eaten.

"Feeling better?"

"A million times," Alice said.

"Good," Russ said. "Now, mind if I give you a lecture?"

Alice sat back and crossed her arms. A dark, depressed looked again changed her lovely face to one of brooding. But she didn't object.

"Let me ask you this," Russ said. "Would you say that Dennis needs you?"

Alice sighed. "Of course he needs me. He needs us all. Stop treating me like a child, Russ."

Alice's defensiveness was not lost on Russ. This was not Alice speaking. She had certainly and firmly constructed an emotional curtain around her. He had to break through.

"Yes, Dennis does need us," Russ said. "Moreover, he depends on us. On our presence. On our support. And on our love. You think he would stop needing all that if, for example, he discovered that I was an alcoholic?"

"No, he wouldn't. And I know exactly where you are leading."

"Tell me."

"No, you started it, Russ; you finish it."

"All right. Steve needs and loves you in the same manner, Alice. He's an intelligent and sensitive guy. Don't you think he'd understand your problem?"

Tears came again to Alice's eyes. "Maybe he would. But he wants to be a father, Russ. He wants it more than—well, maybe even more than he wants me."

"That's ridiculous."

"I know it is. But I can't help how I feel! And I can't take that chance! It would destroy him, I know it would. And it would destroy me."

Russ took her hands, but Alice slipped from his grasp. "Don't worry, I'm in control. I just get crazy whenever I think about it. The best thing for me and Steve, right now, is not to see him. Maybe when he's out of prison for a while, back on his feet, maybe then—"

"You're running away, Alice."

"Yes, I know."

There was a knock on the door.

"You okay?" Russ said to Alice.

"Sure."

"Come in."

Eliot Carrington entered Russ's office. Immediately he turned to Alice.

"Alice! What a surprise. It's terrific to see you."

"Hello, Eliot," Alice said.

Eliot was shocked at Alice's appearance. He looked to Russ with a troubled, questioning expression. Russ shook his head.

"Congratulations," Eliot said to Russ, shaking his hand. "You worked a miracle on my son, and don't you deny it. I'm grateful; we all are."

"You're welcome," Russ said.

Russ respected Eliot, and Eliot was one of the few men whom Russ looked up to. With his piercing brown eyes, tall stature, sharp, dark appearance and agile mind, Eliot was a man who truly knew himself. Eliot and Russ had always had a valuable, serious friendship. Rare, Russ knew, among men.

Eliot said, "You'll never guess who just called me. Iris."

"No kidding," Russ said.

"She was out having brunch with her father, and was so positively ecstatic she had to call and share the news about Dennis with me. With Mac back in town, I have hopes for her."

"Frankly, Eliot," Russ said, "I always wondered why you weren't bitter over what happened between you and Iris."

Eliot waved the air. "We misunderstood each other. Sometimes opposites don't attract."

"Sometimes," Alice said, "sameness isn't the key to success either."

The room was silent for a moment, while Eliot studied Alice, realizing something was desperately wrong that he had not been aware of.

"So, anyway," Eliot said, "Iris said she and Mac would be over within the hour."

"There's nothing much they can do here," Russ said, "but it will be good to see them. Gee, I haven't seen them since, oh, yesterday."

He and Eliot laughed.

Alice rose. She wasn't sticking around if Iris was coming. Iris was another thorn in Alice's life. No, thank you.

"Time to get going," Alice said. "Plenty to do, lots of things to do."

"Take care, Alice," Russ said. "Call me later, okay?"

"I will," Alice said. "Good to see you, Eliot." And she slipped out the door without another word.

When she was gone, Eliot sat on the sofa. "What's wrong with her? She looked horrible."

Russ shook his head and ran his fingers through his curly hair. "She's self-destructing. Part of it is confidential, but the other part is that Steve's being released from prison tomorrow and the last thing on earth Alice wants to do is see him."

On the way down in the elevator, Alice decided to do something she had never before done in times of trouble. Have a stiff drink.

Mac and Iris, father and daughter, were having the best time in years over brunch, much to Mac's surprise, and much to Iris's astonished delight. Somehow, they had fallen into a mutual mood and reached a level of closeness, which was exactly what Iris needed and had hoped for.

"I can't understand it," Mac was saying. "My father was bald, his father was bald, but here I sit with a cranium full of gorgeous silvery locks."

"You're a real good-looker," Iris said, smiling.

"Well, yes, I suppose I am."

"Modest, too."

"Oh, you noticed?"

Iris laughed.

Brunch at the Beaumont was as luscious to view as it was to indulge in. At the far end of the huge, elegant dining room was a table ten yards long displaying everything from scrambled eggs to bagels and lox to crabmeat salad to roast ham. Champagne and coffee and tea flowed by the gallon. Mac had eaten two platefuls and was thinking about a third, while Iris nibbled and picked here and there, constantly monitoring her figure. Neither of them had alcohol, for on both their minds was their imminent visit to Dennis at the hospital.

"You know what you need?" Iris said. "You need a good woman."

Mac nodded. "Or even a bad one."

Iris slapped his arm. "You devil! Is that anything to tell your own daughter?"

Mac smiled. "I was hoping maybe you had some older friends."

"You are too much," Iris said, shaking her head, picking a crumb of her whole-wheat bagel and lifting it to her lips.

Then Iris's gaze swept the room, taking in the grandeur, the sunlight pouring through the tall windows, the crystal chandeliers. Then her eyes widened.

There, halfway across the room, was Rachel. She was sitting at a table with a man in a white laboratory coat. A doctor. They were chatting with much animation. And Rachel looked stunning. Her light-green dress amplified the red highlights of her chestnut hair, which was clean and shiny and bounced whenever she moved. Her eyes sparkled, her face glowed. Iris realized that she and Rachel were about the same age, but suddenly Iris felt much older. She hoped Rachel wouldn't see her.

Rumors about Rachel had been flying all around Bay City, and Iris was a constant and willing receiver. Since Rachel's divorce from Steve, Rachel had made it very clear that she fully intended to make another charge for his affections. But no one really took Rachel seriously. After all, Steve and Alice were now married, and they seemed the perfect couple. Everyone believed that Rachel was merely protecting her pride, spouting vindictive steam because she had lost Steve at the trial. Everyone knew Rachel's boasts were empty and that she was powerless to do a thing. Everyone, that is, except Iris.

Iris fully believed that if Rachel put her mind to it she could get Steve back. All Rachel needed was a break. Beside Rachel, Iris felt like a weakling.

And now Rachel had seen them.

Iris turned quickly to Mac. "Let's go, okay?"

Mac, chewing, looked at her. "Now? I haven't finished my haddock."

Now Rachel was kissing the young doctor on the cheek. He was leaving, and Rachel was heading toward Iris, smoothing her dress over her long thighs as she came.

There was no escape. Iris threw back her shoulders and patted her lips with her linen napkin.

"Iris," Rachel said, approaching, "what a pleasant surprise."

"Believe me, I was more surprised than you were," Iris said. And she said nothing else.

Mac looked from woman to woman, then held his gaze on Rachel for a second. He hurriedly pulled a fishbone from between his lips, laid it on the edge of his plate, then cleared his throat.

"Aren't you going to introduce me?" Mac said.

"Rachel, this is my father, Mackenzie Cory. Mac, this is Rachel Frame—or is it Matthews? Or Davis? I'm sorry, Rachel, I haven't been keeping track."

Mac rose, his napkin slipping off his lap to the floor in his haste. He took Rachel's offered hand and shook it once. "Very pleased to meet you, Rachel. Please sit down, join us."

"Thank you," Rachel said.

Mac held the chair for Rachel as she sat down, his eyes moving up and down her back. Mac regained his seat, ignoring the napkin on the floor.

"Allow me to clear up the mystery for you, Iris," Rachel said with a smile that included Mac. "Obviously I'm not using the surname Frame, since my ex-husband has remarried. Matthews, as you well know, hails from another ex of mine, dear Russ, and though I was using that for a while, I have shucked that also. I was considering using the name Hooplefrog. What do you think?"

It caught Mac by surprise, and he coughed and then laughed loudly. Iris's face glowed beet red.

"A fine, upstanding name," Mac said.

Rachel was laughing, too, at Iris's expense, and she once again offered her hand to Mac, who took it.

"Rachel Davis, Mr. Cory, and I'm very pleased to meet you."

"Likewise," Mac said. "And if you don't call me Mac, I'll start feeling like your father, too."

Mac and Rachel exchanged smiles and stares. Mac couldn't keep his eyes off her. Though Rachel seemed to be about Iris's age, perhaps a few years older, she seemed to possess a maturity that Iris lacked. A self-assurance. And, oh yes, Mac realized, a lot of dangerous spunk. This woman, Mac thought, was one to be reckoned with. Still, there was something in Rachel's glittering eyes that spoke of hidden pain.

Rachel laid her hand on Iris's arm. Iris tolerated it. "Iris, I just heard the terrific news about Dennis's operation. I'm really happy, after so long, that it turned out this well."

"Thank you," Iris said. Rachel seemed sincere, and Iris lost a good measure of her defensiveness.

"May I get you anything?" Mac said to Rachel.

"No, thank you, I'm stuffed."

"Weren't you going after another plate?" Iris said to Mac.

Mac sat a bit straighter and pulled in his stomach. "Who, me? Oh, no. Couldn't fit it in. Besides, I'll blow two weeks of exercises. Gotta watch the caloric intake."

"Oh, you exercise?" Rachel asked.

"Sure do," Mac said proudly. "Every day. It's the key to long life, and I've still got a lot of life to live."

Iris felt like crawling under the table. Her father was making a fool of himself. Obviously, he was stricken by Rachel, showing off, acting like a kid on his first date. Rachel probably thought he was an old fool.

Iris stood up. "Excuse me a moment. I must powder my nose. Join me, Rachel?"

"No, I think you can handle your nose all by yourself," Rachel said.

Rachel was in top form, Iris thought. And she left the table and headed across the room. Her analyst had told her to avoid stressful situations when possible. Nervous breakdowns had a way of recurring if you didn't monitor yourself.

"I've been in town only a few weeks," Mac said. "Moved back to keep an eye on Dennis and my daughter."

"I'm really glad the news is good," Rachel said. "And welcome to Bay City. We need someone sane around here to keep an eye on all of us."

As soon as Iris had left the table, Mac noticed that Rachel's sharp attitude vanished. Now she didn't quite know what to do with herself, as if something was on her mind, something that hurt her deeply. Mac's heart immediately went out to her, in all her beauty and complexity.

"How long have you been divorced?" Mac asked. And he knew right away that that was the wrong question to ask. He would ask Iris about it later.

Rachel's large blue eyes seemed to grow darker. She tossed back her silky hair and propped her chin on her fist, polished nails shining. "Divorce is divorce," Rachel said. "It's never fun and it's never easy, no matter what the reason."

"Right you are," Mac said. "I'm sorry for prying."

What Rachel saw in Mac's eyes and heard in his voice was sympathy. Sympathy was something Rachel was not accustomed to.

"Tell me about yourself," Rachel said.

"Glad to," Mac said. "First, I'm rich. Filthy rich. Might as well confess that right now."

Rachel laughed. "And I'm very glad you did. It's best to know the worst about a person so you can appreciate the good."

"How true!"

And they chatted on.

When Iris returned to the table, Mac and Rachel barely noticed. The closeness Iris and her father had been sharing before Rachel's invasion was gone. Iris felt as if Rachel had stolen something from her.

"Excuse me," Iris said. "I think it's time we get to the hospital."

"I agree," Mac said. "It was a pleasure meeting you, Rachel."

"Likewise."

They shook hands.

Iris thought, *Mac's really turning on the charm.* Iris was embarrassed for him, and angry at Rachel for ruining her morning.

All three stood up at once.

Then Rachel said, "Isn't that Alice Frame?"

Mac and Iris looked where Rachel was nodding. Yes, it was indeed Alice, looking absolutely terrible. She entered the restaurant hesitantly, jerking her gaze this way and that, hair askew, dark circles under her eyes. She took a few steps toward the bar, then suddenly stopped. She had seen Rachel and Iris. Alice spun around and rushed out of the restaurant.

"That *was* Alice Frame, wasn't it?" Rachel said.

Iris, who had been harboring hate for Alice for some time, blaming her for the breakup of her marriage, was not disappointed to see Alice not looking her best.

"It was," Iris said. "I've heard that Steve's going to prison really took the wind out of her sails."

"Oh, really," Rachel said. Now, here was a piece of news she had somehow missed.

"Iris," Mac said, "you really have to catch me up on all this intrigue."

"Yes, I must," Iris said. She looked pointedly at Rachel. "Believe me, I'll spill it all."

Rachel glared at her.

Mac, the perpetual peacemaker, couldn't stand parting company on a bad note. "Listen," he said, "I have a terrific idea. Rachel, why don't you come with us to the hospital? Afterward, I'll take us all out to lunch."

"No, I really couldn't," Rachel said. Rachel knew Russ would be there, and he was one ex-husband she could do without seeing.

Iris was greatly relieved. Mac had been practically drooling all over Rachel, and Iris wanted to see her son surrounded by family, a family that desperately needed a peaceful reunion.

"But I insist," Mac said.

"Mac, Rachel has said she can't come," Iris said. "I'm sure she's extremely busy."

Rachel couldn't resist. Iris obviously did not want Rachel along. And since Rachel was still steaming after Iris's earlier barb, this was an opportunity Rachel could not let pass.

"I hate to see a grown man beg," Rachel said. "I accept your kind invitation."

Mac absolutely glowed. He offered one arm to Rachel, who took it and hugged it immediately, then he offered the other arm to Iris, who didn't move. He offered it again, and Iris, humiliated and furious, snatched it and squeezed.

Mac, beaming, walked them out. "This is my lucky day," Mac said. "The two most beautiful women in Bay City, and I've got them." Mac had spoken those words only to Rachel.

Chapter Four
To Love Again

Winter for Lenore was indeed a wonderland. Her world changed, and she changed with it.

It began that October evening at the party with Robert Delaney, and it continued when Robert picked her up promptly at six-thirty for dinner and a Broadway show.

When she opened her front door, the sight of Robert surprised her. Though it had been only two weeks since she'd seen him at the party, she had forgotten what a powerful physical presence he possessed.

"It's me," he said, standing on the porch in a dashing, calf-length black overcoat. In one hand he held a dozen red roses, in the other a pair of leather gloves. Behind him a chocolate-brown limousine waited. His dazzling smile brought to Lenore not memories of their one fabulous evening, but remembrances of her surprisingly strong feelings.

"Come in," she said, shivering in a cool rush of air. "I'll be ready in three minutes."

Robert stepped inside. "You look breathtaking."

Lenore brushed at the front of her new blue dress. "You really think so?"

"I do. And what a lovely house," he said. "I remember your saying you fell in love with it at first sight. I don't blame you. They don't make structures like this anymore. I don't even build them. Do you know how much it would cost to construct one of these today? Don't ask." He held out the roses. "These are for you."

Lenore gingerly accepted the roses. She hadn't received flowers in—she couldn't recall the last time. She was moved and thanked him shyly. She immediately ran for a tall crystal vase and water. She displayed his gift, arranging the roses carefully, in the center of the living room on the Italian marble coffee table.

"Here, let me take your coat," Lenore said.

"I'll handle it. Don't trouble yourself. Go on, finish whatever you have to do. I have reservations for dinner at six forty-five."

Lenore turned toward the staircase in a sudden burst of enthusiasm. "Be right down."

When Lenore was halfway up, Robert called, "Say, where's Wally?"

"Oh. He's at the sitter's. I took him over early."

"Too bad. I wanted to meet the boy. Next time, I guess."

"Make yourself comfortable."

Lenore hurried upstairs. She could actually hear her heart beating. She sat at her dressing table to put the final touches on her makeup.

She didn't want Wally to meet Robert. Not yet. That's why she had taken Wally over early. What she was feeling was unclear, but the thought of the two of them meeting frightened her. Who knows what Wally would think? Would he be jealous? Would he withdraw? It didn't matter. There was simply no point in the two of them meeting right now. It might or might not hurt to bring them together, so the safest thing was to just wait.

Lenore applied the last of her lip gloss, stood up, then paused. Or was there something else behind hiding Wally from Robert? *Yes, that's exactly it,* she decided. *I'm hiding my son. Maybe I'm afraid of the competition for Wally's attention. What a horrible thought.* Lenore had been aware ever since Walter's death that, sooner or later, she would have to provide a male influence in Wally's life. But it was far too early now, right? What if Robert and Wally got along terrifically? What if she and Robert split up? Wally would be crushed. And then there would probably be another man, and another man. A situation like that could ruin a boy. Couldn't it? Or would it ruin her?

She stared hard at herself in the mirror. "Oh, shut up and get going."

She took one last look to make sure everything was in place. Two hours at the hairdresser's and her flowing dark-blond hair played gently on her shoulders and around her face perfectly. Her blue eyes sparkled. And her figure in the new dress, she decided, bordered on voluptuousness. It had been quite a while since Lenore had looked at herself and thought, *there's a sexy woman.* She did so now, and happily turned and soon reentered the living room.

Robert wasn't there.

For a second, she panicked. "Robert?"

"In here." His voice came from another room. Then he walked out of the study. "Sorry, I couldn't resist exploring. I'm not being nosy, honest. I'm an architect, remember? This house is one piece of fine work. Solid. It'll last for another hundred years. And I'm boring you silly."

"No, you're not." It bothered Lenore that he felt free to wander around her home, her sanctuary. Lenore was possessive of her things, her space, but she fought the feelings back and snatched her coat out of the closet.

Robert took it from her, helped her into it, then left his hands on her shoulders for a moment before turning her toward him.

"Hungry?" he said.

Lenore nodded, certain he was about to kiss her, trying to decide what to do about it.

He reached for the doorknob and flung open the door. "Your carriage awaits. Let's be off."

"Let's."

Dinner was marvelous, full of animated conversation. Lenore wondered how they came up with so many things to talk about. She found herself involved in conversation on topics she didn't even realize she was interested in. She just let Robert bend and weave the dialogue and she followed happily. She liked allowing him to take charge. She liked reacting, instead of being the one to initiate things, a position Lenore was uncomfortable in.

She also liked looking at him, studying his face as he talked in that mock-serious manner. His hands, too, she liked. Strong but sensitive, well-formed and manicured. He used his hands often when he spoke, and often she found them touching her arm, her shoulder, or resting on her warm wrist.

On to the theater they went. The musical was

touted as being history-making, the biggest extravaganza to hit Broadway in years. The signs implied that they were extremely lucky to have such a touring show arrive in the Bay City area.

The show was loud and wisecracking, bursting with song-and-dance numbers every five minutes. The final curtain was greeted with thundering applause by the four hundred people attending. The cast members took their curtain calls with smug, superior expressions on their faces. They were loved and they deserved it, their manner said.

In silence, Robert and Lenore walked arm in arm back toward the limo. The driver was waiting beside the open rear door. Before they entered, Robert paused and turned toward Lenore.

"The show stunk, didn't it?" he said.

Lenore nodded. "Awful. Juvenile."

"Ignorant. Insulting. Simplistic."

They looked into each other's eyes and burst into hearty laughter. With one strong arm, he pulled her to him and gave her a hug. Then they climbed into the car and the driver closed the door.

"Well, I suppose it's time to pick up Wally," Robert said.

"Actually, no."

"No?"

"He's staying at his friend's house. He asked to stay overnight and I said okay."

Lenore hoped she didn't make that sound like an invitation for Robert to spend the night. In fact, she hadn't even planned on telling Robert. She thought she'd just go home and spend a quiet night alone for a change. But she was having such a great time, she was not yet ready for the evening to end.

"That's the best news yet," Robert said. He checked his watch. Lenore noticed it was an eight-thousand-dollar gold Rolex. It suddenly dawned on her that Robert was a rich man. Probably a very rich man. "It is now ten-thirty," he said. "Where to? Hungry?"

"After that meal we had?" she said. "No, not hungry."

"Then I suggest we work some of it off. A little dancing. Some wine. Sound good?"

"Wonderful."

Robert lifted the phone and spoke to the driver. "Moonlight Cabaret, Tom. Thanks."

The driver nodded and they were off.

Robert leaned sideways and touched shoulders with Lenore. The pleasing, powdery scent of his cologne filled her head. "You're terrific and much-needed company, Lenore."

She had to part her lips to breathe. "Ditto," she said.

He faced her. "You're quickly becoming more than that, you know."

"I—"

His lips fell upon hers, fitting perfectly. She closed her eyes as he pressed gently. The skin on her back and chest goose-bumped, then grew warm. When she lifted her hand to the back of his head, his arm moved around to her side. They embraced, the kiss working magic on both of them; then, together, they slowly released each other. Their lips were the last to part. Lenore relaxed back into the seat, unable to think for a moment, savoring the beginnings of passion, the desires she hadn't felt for years, realizing the joys she had been missing.

"You know," Robert finally said, "we have Janet to thank for it all."

Lenore looked at him mischievously, then slapped his leg. "Oh! You liar! I forgot all about that!" She slapped him again.

Robert threw his head back and laughed, then drew his arm around her and kissed her on the cheek. She settled into his chest, heart racing, wondering what lay ahead.

Wally met Robert on Thanksgiving day. All week, Lenore had been a nervous wreck. She had told Wally about Robert, who he was, what he did, and tried to explain a bit about how she felt. Wally listened quietly, and Lenore wasn't sure whether he understood or not.

Lenore toyed with the idea of hiring someone to do the cooking and serving, but decided against it. Instead, she threw herself into the preparations for the meal. When the clock struck noon on Thanksgiving day and the doorbell rang, Lenore had to wipe her hands on her dress three times before gripping the doorknob. Before she opened the door, Lenore looked back at Wally. He stood in the center of the living room, hair combed, clothes pressed, with an expression of fear on his face. Had she overdone the whole thing? Too late now.

Lenore opened the door. Robert stood there with a smile.

"Happy Thanksgiving, darling," he said. He moved toward Lenore.

She whispered, "Please, don't kiss me or anything. He's watching."

Robert winked.

"Come on in, and happy Thanksgiving to you, too," Lenore said loudly, realizing she sounded phony and tense and shrill.

Robert stepped into the room, looked at Wally and grinned widely. "So, you're the famous Wally, eh?"

Wally did nothing.

Robert walked directly over to him. Lenore stood where she was, discovered her fingers were in her mouth and threw her hands behind her back.

"My name's Bob," Robert said, squatting down in front of Wally.

Wally said nothing.

"Say hello, Wally," Lenore said.

"Hi," Wally said, moving back a step.

Robert smiled, then he whispered to Wally. "You know, your mom warned me about you. She said you were really ugly but, you know, you're not bad-looking at all."

"She did not," Wally said.

"Well, maybe I'm wrong," Robert said. "How old are you, Wally?"

"Six."

"Gee, that's too bad. I guess you're too young."

Wally's eyes widened.

"See," Robert said to Wally, "on the way over here, I bought some things, but now I guess you're too young to have them."

"What are they?" Wally said.

"Just a few of these." Robert took five comic books out of his coat pocket. "Batman, Superman, Spider Man. No, you're too young to be interested in these."

"I am not!" Wally said. "Batman's my favorite!"

"No, you're just saying that to be nice."

"No, I'm not!"

"You're not nice?" Robert said.

Wally laughed, lunging at the comics Robert was now holding behind his back. "Gimme 'em!"

"Say please," Lenore said, laughing.

"Too bad you're so young," Robert said, dodging the giggling boy.

"Please!"

Robert surrendered the comics and made an instant friend.

The day was a winner, the meal delicious and Lenore couldn't help thinking if this was the start of a whole new family for her.

A couple of times a week and most weekends, Lenore and Robert continued their whirlwind courtship. From drives in the country to a fabulous and extravagant weekend in Los Angeles to quiet and happy evenings just sitting around the house and chatting, their relationship blossomed and thrived on Robert's self-assurance and the melting away of most of Lenore's fears.

From time to time it annoyed her that Robert was kind of bossy. Mostly they did only the things Robert wanted to do. They had terrific times, but if Lenore wanted to shop for herself she usually found herself alone. She would have liked Robert's opinions, but he always begged off going. But, she told herself, these were little things. Nothing to be worried about at all.

Their good times continued. Lenore visited Robert's plush offices, with rows of designer's tables, stacks of blueprints, photos of awesome and beautiful buildings and houses Robert had designed and built. He was proud of his work, of his business, and Lenore was proud for him.

Lenore was realizing that Robert could give her everything she ever needed or wanted.

A cloud of disappointment entered Lenore's life

when Robert said he couldn't see her and Wally for Christmas. He had promised his parents that he'd fly to Cincinnati to visit for the holiday weekend. He offered to bring them along, but Lenore felt her place was with Wally in their own home, with their own tree.

Christmas was joyous, and Lenore and Wally spent their time visiting friends, sled-riding and making snowmen. But inside, with Robert suddenly absent, Lenore felt a hollowness and emptiness. And the old doubts and fears began to resurface.

Would Robert really return? Was this his way of making a clean exit? Would this turn out to be the worst time of her life? And what about Wally? Had she made a grave error bringing Robert into their lives?

On New Year's Eve, with Lenore having refused to go anywhere, she was at the greatest depth of her depression. Then the most remarkable and unexpected thing happened. Without a call, without warning, the doorbell rang and there was Robert, grinning from ear to handsome ear. His arms were piled high with presents, all festively wrapped.

"Ho, ho, ho!" Robert said, pretending to stumble into the house, sending Wally into shrieks of laughter. "Santa's a little late this year, but better late than never!"

Amen, Lenore thought.

Robert unloaded his gifts on the sofa and immediately, for the first time in front of Wally, he embraced Lenore and kissed her deeply. Wally was too busy looking for his presents to notice.

Wally was sound asleep upstairs when the clock struck midnight. As she had done with the dawn of every new year, Lenore cried. She fell into Robert's arms with tears for the past, for the future, for hopes unrealized and dreams yet to come true. Robert tenderly kissed away her tears, then lifted her chin and kissed her puffy lips.

Lenore smiled. "I feel like a child. Happens every New Year's. It's silly."

"Not silly," Robert said. "It's beautiful." He kissed her again.

"You know what I was thinking while you were away?"

"What?"

"I was thinking," she said, "that you would never come back."

"You should know better."

"I do now."

"Good. Because, I'm sorry to say, I have to leave town on business the day after tomorrow."

"Oh, Bob. Do you?"

"It's the fine-arts complex I'm designing in New Jersey. Seems a zoning problem has come up, and the goons out there still can't make up their minds whether they want three theaters or two theaters and an extra art gallery. Driving me crazy."

"How long will you be gone?"

"Well, this first time, I'll be gone only a week."

Lenore sat up. "This first time?"

"I have to go and straighten out this mess, then I'll be back here, but I'll be busy drafting blueprints for the new requirements. Then I have to go back out to finalize."

Lenore fell silent.

Robert tried to hug her but she was stiff. "Oh, come on, Lenore. This has nothing to do with you. It's the work I do, the way I have to do business, it's my career. You'll miss me, eh?"

"Yes, and you don't have to be so smug about it." Lenore cracked a smile. She knew she was being silly.

"Oh, we forgot the champagne!"

Robert leaped up, uncorked the bottle and poured two sparkling glasses. Lenore rose and took one from him.

"Happy New Year," she said, clinking his glass.

"To us," Robert said.

"Yes, to us."

They drank.

Lenore saw Robert only twice during the next month. His words during his many phone calls were reassuring, but she still missed him desperately. He had become a part of her, of her life, of how she spent her time.

Then the project in New Jersey was well in hand, and Lenore and Robert decided to celebrate with a lavish dinner, then a walk through the snow.

On a footbridge in the center of Roosevelt Park, Robert suddenly stopped and turned Lenore toward him. With large snowflakes dotting Robert's wavy hair, he gazed deeply into her eyes and said, "I love you, Lenore. I've never been more certain of anything."

"And I love you, too, Bob," she said. "I've known it for a while now. But I'm scared. Not a lot; a little."

"We have time, and plenty of it. And we have each other."

They kissed, then continued their walk.

To Lenore, it seemed too perfect to be true. But it was true, it was happening and her feelings were honest and open. And, after all she'd been through, she felt she deserved it.

Chapter Five
Victories and Defeats

The cool March morning was warming under a brilliant noontime sun when Mac, Rachel and Iris entered the hospital lobby.

"These places give me the creeps," Rachel said. "I've never been good at visiting hospitals."

"Wait until you're in one," Iris said quietly. All knew she was referring to her nervous breakdown.

"Iris, I wasn't talking about insane asylums," Rachel said.

Mac, to break the ice between the two women, laughed forcibly. "You two should perform a stand-up comedy routine. I swear, you're great together."

"Buddy-buddy," Iris snapped.

They got their visitors' passes at the main desk, entered the large steel elevator and soon found themselves walking toward Russ Matthews' office.

Iris's mind moved off Rachel and filled with thoughts of her son, Dennis. Poor little Dennis. She hadn't been a very good mother to him through all this, but she was determined to be a good one now.

This was a new beginning, a new start for mother and child. But the first step toward her son must take her past Eliot. Somehow, she had to make peace with her ex-husband. She could never forgive him for chasing after Alice—Iris was still convinced he had —but that was now history. So since she couldn't forgive, she would try her best to forget. Having Mac there helped greatly, boosted her courage and gave her something solid to fall back on. Yes, she could handle it. She swallowed hard, tried to compose herself and followed her father into Russ's office.

After handshakes and hesitant hellos, Russ said that if they could wait fifteen minutes they all could take a quick look in on Dennis. All settled in to wait, and the strange reunion began.

"It's good to see you, Mac," Eliot said.

"Good to be seen, Eliot. You look well, healthy. How's the writing going?"

"Very well, indeed."

Eliot had yet to say anything to his ex-wife, Iris. She noticed he eyed her suspiciously, probably waiting for her to blow up, or cry, or break down.

"Eliot," Iris said, "how's Dennis?"

"Out of recovery and into a room. He's still under, though, but Russ says everything looks positive for a full recovery."

"We're very lucky, you know that," Iris said.

Eliot smiled. "We are, Iris."

Mac was grateful for the temporary peace between them, and he moved his gaze across the room to Rachel. He studied her, observing every intriguing mannerism with keen curiosity.

Rachel was talking with her ex-husband Russ, who

had taken an obviously defensive posture on the edge of his desk, arms and legs crossed. He thought he was acting detached and in control.

"I was sorry to hear of your divorce from Steve Frame," Russ said.

"Were you really?" Rachel said, hand poised on cocked hip. She suddenly wondered what on earth she was doing there.

"I'm serious. You haven't had it easy lately, and I am sincerely concerned."

"Well, thank you, Russ. You always were quite lavish with your concern."

Russ shook his head. "I see you haven't changed."

"Oh, I've changed, Russ. It's your vision that hasn't improved."

Rachel left Russ and moved over to stand beside Mac.

"Eliot," she said, "did Iris tell you whom we saw this morning? Alice Frame. She walked into the Beaumont looking terminally horrible, then turned and walked right back out again."

"Really?" Eliot said thoughtfully. "I hope she pulls herself together soon. You know, Steve is being released tomorrow."

"So I've heard," Rachel said. "Russ, what's your considered opinion of Alice's condition?"

Russ walked up and addressed everyone. "Her condition is nothing to make fun of. She has problems and let's leave it at that."

"I agree," Eliot said.

Iris realized that Eliot knew something about Alice that she did not. This she couldn't tolerate. "What kind of problems?"

"Iris, this is no place for gossip," Eliot said.

"Oh, Eliot," Rachel said, "we're not gossiping. We're sincerely concerned. Frankly, I don't know why Alice would be upset about Steve's being released tomorrow. If I were her I'd be ecstatic."

Iris was losing patience. "As I recall, Rachel, you had your chance at ecstasy."

Rachel closed her eyes and huffed. Mac felt like kicking his daughter. He shot her a stern look, and Iris was shocked to see that he was taking Rachel's side.

"Look," Russ said, "Alice's problems are none of our business."

"But they seem to be yours," Rachel said.

"Yes, she's been up to see me. There's much more to her problems than I can tell you."

"So you've been seeing her professionally?" Rachel asked.

Eliot rose. "I think it's time to take a look in at Dennis, don't you?"

Mac rose also. "I'm for that."

Russ checked his watch, noting that the watchband felt tight. He was heated and upset. "Actually, I think we should wait a few more minutes. He's still being attended to."

"In that case," Rachel said, "I must say good-bye. It seems I'm an upsetting influence in the room. This is a happy time, and I'm sorry if I put a damper on things."

"You really haven't, you know," Mac said.

In a quieter tone, Rachel said to Mac, "I truly am glad to have met you, Mac. I enjoyed our talk and found you entertaining company."

"Thank you. Are you sure you won't reconsider lunch?"

"I honestly can't," Rachel said, suddenly in a rush. "It was good to see all of you again, even you, Russ. Bye-bye." And Rachel left the room and closed the door.

Immediately Iris felt herself relaxing.

"Remarkable woman," Mac said, staring at the closed door.

"Not quite how I'd describe her," Russ said, moving back around his desk and sitting down.

"I don't know," Mac said. "I have no idea what she's been up to in the past, of course, but I liked her. She's a woman with a heart who needs a good shoulder to cry on."

Iris laughed. "Mac, you couldn't be more wrong. She's a selfish opportunist, and everyone in this room knows it."

"Enough," Russ said. "Leave it be."

Mac scratched his head. "Maybe someone ought to explain to me what I'm missing. Sure, Rachel's kind of ornery, but somewhere along the line I think she's been hurt deeply. It's obvious to me. She's out there all alone now, fighting for survival the only way she knows how."

"Mac," Iris said, "you're romanticizing. You met her for the first time mere hours ago. Really, you don't know what you're talking about."

"Maybe not," Mac said. "But I'm curious, and I wouldn't mind finding out."

My God, Iris thought, *my father's captivated*. She felt her blood pressure rising. Old jealous feelings surfaced and she wrung her hands, trying to squeeze some control into her mind. Just when Iris had thought she was beginning to break through with her father, along came Rachel to distract him. She was certain Rachel

71

was doing it only because she knew it irritated Iris. But if there was one thing Rachel couldn't get enough of it was attention. And if there was going to be a battle, this was one battle Iris vowed not to lose.

For now, Iris thought, the less said about Rachel the better.

"Do you think we can see Dennis now?" Iris said.

Russ again checked his watch. "I suppose so. But remember, he's still anesthetized. He won't even know you are there."

Soon they were crowded around the door of the intensive care ward. Russ would not let them into the room. Dennis looked so tiny in the adult bed, Iris thought. So helpless. It was a sad and pitiful sight, but she knew, she hoped, the result would be joyous. Soon, Dennis would be awake, sitting up, and maybe later walking through the park holding her hand. Holding both her hand and Mac's. A family. She now wanted it more than anything on earth.

Rachel had not left the hospital. What luck, she thought, to have gone up to see Russ with everyone. What incredible luck. This, she suspected, could possibly be the missing link in the chain that would bind Steve Frame to her forever.

She was seeking Dr. George Harrison. At brunch, he'd said he had to make rounds, so he would still be in the hospital and not in his office on the other side of town.

She knew he'd be somewhere on the third floor, and when she passed the reception desk, there he was, bent over while filling out forms, his longish red hair hanging sexily over his handsome brow.

"George," Rachel said.

He straightened up. "Rachel. What are you doing here?"

"I have to talk with you."

"Just a sec. Have some supply orders to sign." He signed a few more papers, stuck his pen in his top pocket with three others, then turned to her. "What about?"

It was far too crowded to talk where they were, so Rachel took his arm and led him to a corner by the elevators.

"I need a favor, George, a big favor," Rachel said. "And I promise you, you won't be sorry if you can swing it for me." She scratched his upper arm with her red fingernails.

George was interested. "Speak, and I shall obey."

"George, what do you know about Alice Frame?"

George shrugged. "That's a tough one. I haven't been working with Russ too long. What is it you want to know?"

"Nothing major," Rachel said. "Just what's been happening lately. Any problems she might have had."

"Oh, if that's all it is," George said, "you've come to the right man. Just did some filing on Alice Frame a few moments ago. I couldn't resist taking a little look-see."

"Terrific. Tell me."

"Alice has some psychological problems. Nothing serious, just adjustment-type troubles. Depression, that kind of stuff. Russ thinks it has to do with her husband's being in prison."

"I know all that," Rachel said. "What else?"

"Well, the rest is confidential."

"That, you dummy, is exactly what I want to know," she said playfully. She tugged on the sleeve of his lab coat then ran her hand up his arm.

"I could get canned for this, you know."

"I know, but you won't because you're too smart. Besides, you're doing it for love."

"Correction," George said. "I'm doing it for lust. All right. Alice is barren. She can't have kids. Russ thinks this is really messing her up. Evidently, she hasn't told Steve, and now she's lost all courage and thinks she's something less than human."

"That's great, couldn't be better. Now, George, I want a copy of that file."

"Now?"

"Now."

He looked long into Rachel's seductive blue eyes. "Be right back." And George abruptly turned and walked swiftly down the hall.

Rachel paced.

In less than five minutes, George came down the hall with a box of candy in his hand. He gave it to Rachel.

"Aw, you shouldn't have," Rachel said. "But where's the file?"

George was flushed. "Inside, folded. Now get out of here and I'll see you later."

She pecked him on the cheek. "Thanks, hon, you will not regret this."

The elevator door suddenly opened, like fate. Rachel entered. The door closed.

Sucker, she thought.

The next morning, at dawn, Steve Frame was released from prison. Newspaper reporters yakked questions,

TV cameras rolled, friends and family were waiting with smiles and hugs and Steve searched the crowd for a very important face.

"What was it like on the inside?" a newsman asked.

"It was prison, what do you think it was like?" Steve said.

"How did you spend your time?"

"Slowly."

"Was the food good?"

"No."

"Did you contact your office while you were in?"

"Yes."

"Where's Mrs. Frame?"

Silence.

"Yeah, where's his wife?"

Suddenly, the news hounds had another story to chew on.

Steve Frame entered the waiting limousine and sped away. He was biting his nails, something he hadn't done since he was a kid.

When he arrived at their mansion, Alice wasn't there. A servant told him she had not been there for days and that he did not know where she was staying.

Panic grew and gripped Steve's throat. He made many calls, trying to track Alice down, to no avail. Even Russ didn't know where to find her, although he told Steve not to worry.

Don't worry. What a laugh.

At first he was deeply hurt, but then he realized that he had half expected this to be the case. Alice had not visited him once while he was in prison. He had sent messages to her but had received no answers. And now she had vanished. But why?

The phone rang, again and again and again; each

ring was like a twisting knife. News reporters. Cranks. His office.

Get yourself together, Steve said to himself. *One thing at a time. You're out, at long last. The nightmare is over. Your wife obviously doesn't want to see you. Why?* That he couldn't answer. The answer could come only from her, and right now he did not know where she was. No one did.

All right, then. What now? Shower. Dress. Get over to the office. From the office he could send out feelers, get private investigators if he had to. His office was his control center, and from there Steve Frame knew he wielded tremendous power.

While in the shower, Steve surprised himself by lurching into deep, heartfelt sobs.

Everyone at the office cheered when Steve entered. They had balloons and banners and champagne.

"Thank you all," he said. "Thank you." And he walked into his office and closed the door.

Everyone there understood. The poor guy practically owned the world, and he couldn't control or find his own wife. They felt sorry for him, and yet they were a slight bit pleased, as if getting revenge.

Inside his office, Steve's five top men were waiting for him. They crowded around him, shaking his hand, patting his shoulder.

"Good to have you back," Willis, his younger brother, said.

"Likewise," Gil Tunney, V.P., said. "It's been crazy without you."

Steve strode behind his desk and faced them all. "Gents, I am sure you are all aware of my personal problems. I'd appreciate some time to straighten them out. I'll call when I need you."

"Right," Willis said. "But there's just one thing—"

"No, Willis. Please, give me time."

"But, Steve—"

"Willis, do I have to throw you out by the seat of your pants? I haven't done that since we were kids, but I'm just upset enough now to do it."

Willis grew red. When he turned to leave he was glad to see that the others had already gone. With as much dignity as he could muster, he walked through the door and closed it firmly.

Steve gave a huge sigh and rested his arms on the desk top.

"Welcome back, Steve," said a voice from the far corner.

Steve whirled. Sitting there with a box of candy on her lap was Rachel.

"How'd you get in here?"

Rachel laughed. "Your brother was trying to tell you I was here, but you wouldn't give him the chance."

Steve sat in his leather desk chair. "I need some privacy, Rachel. I can't deal with you now."

"I'm sorry, Steve, I really am," Rachel said, moving over and taking a chair across from his desk. "I wish I'd seen Alice so I could tell you where she is."

"I'll bet you do."

"I've been doing a lot of thinking while you were in prison, Steve. I made a few decisions and I don't hold any grudges."

"That's good to know. Is that all?"

"No, it isn't. We've known each other a long time, through better and worse. Through it all. I thought maybe you might like to talk with someone who understands."

He looked up at her. She was a stunning woman, he couldn't deny it. And the look on her face right now was one of security, possibly even caring. She knew him, all right, and he did need to talk.

"What is wrong with her?" Steve said. "She didn't visit me in prison, didn't write, not there to meet me when I got out, not home either. People tell me she looks horrible, but that's all I get. I just wish I knew what was going on."

"Did you call Russ?"

"Yes, but he couldn't or wouldn't tell me a thing."

Rachel said quietly, "Would you like me to?"

"What do you mean?" His suspicions shot to the surface.

"I know why Alice won't see you, Steve. And it isn't very good news, I'm afraid." Rachel thoroughly enjoyed her situation. She had him right where she wanted him.

"How would you know anything?" Steve said, then raised his palm. "I take it back. If anyone knows anything about anything in this town, it is you. All right, what do you know?"

Rachel carefully opened the candy box and took out the Xerox copy of the medical file. She slid it onto Steve's desk, making him stretch out and reach for it.

Steve read, and as he did, his eyes widened and his face paled. Soon, he let the papers fall and looked up at Rachel.

"I'm sorry, Steve, I really am. I can't tell you how I got that file, but I swear to you that it is authentic."

Steve remained silent, staring at Rachel unbelievingly.

"The horrible truth is that Alice can't have children, Steve. She's lied to you all along. And when you went to prison and she still hadn't told you, it destroyed her. How could she ever confess to you a terrible thing like that after you had spent four months in jail? She couldn't, so she broke down. She tricked you into marrying her, Steve. She betrayed you and your fatherhood for her own selfish interest in becoming your wife. It has ruined her, and I don't want to see her ruin you, too."

Steve rose, ran his hand through his hair and turned to face the window.

"Steve, it's fate, don't you see that? Despite everything, we were meant for each other. We're two of a kind. I still love you, Steve, and I'm willing to take you back."

Steve slowly turned around. Rachel quickly rose at the sight of his face, the unbridled anger.

"I want you out of here now," he said in a quiet but frighteningly intense tone.

"Don't you see what she's done?" Rachel pleaded.

"All I see is that you are the lowest, most despicable poor excuse for a woman I have ever known."

Steve began to move toward her from behind his desk. Veins stood out brilliantly from his neck. His breaths were heavy, his teeth gnashing. Rage at being locked up in prison had been simmering for months. Now he was about to explode, and he had no idea what he would do.

Rachel backed up, with growing terror in her eyes, her hand already reaching backward in search of the doorknob.

"Take it easy, Steve. I was only trying to help."

"I swear to God, Rachel, if you say one more word I'll strangle you right here. Get out. Now. If I ever see you again I'll bribe every official in the state and risk everything to have you put behind bars for the rest of your miserable life."

He strode straight at her.

Rachel shrieked, spun around, flung open the door and ran down the hall.

Steve grasped the edge of the door and slammed it hard. He bashed his fist onto the door frame. He swore, then kicked a chair and watched it tumble into the wall. Then he tried to get control of himself.

So that was it, he thought. The poor darling, poor Alice. Work could wait. Right now he had to pull his life together. He'd find Alice if it took a week, a month.

He thought about calling in a private investigator, but then he got a hunch of his own. He raced out of the office, down the hall, through a wall of hanging balloons, and was soon out of the building, racing after his future.

Steve knew as soon as he pulled into the driveway that Alice was at home. He'd suspected that she would return once she had seen him leave for the office. Or maybe she had been in the house the whole time. It didn't matter.

Steve tore through the front door, up the wide staircase and down the hall to their bedroom. He slowed and stood filling the doorway.

Alice was packing. Two suitcases were gaping on the bed, and she was frantically stuffing clothes into them, crying all the while.

He took a moment just to look at her. He had not seen the woman he loved for four long months. And this was not the Alice he remembered. Drawn, pale, with hair unkempt, this was a woman at the end of her rope. His heart went out to her. It was up to him.

"Alice," Steve said softly.

Alice reacted as if someone had screamed. She jerked back, losing her balance, and sat hard on the edge of the bed. "Oh, no," she said when she saw him.

Steve took a few steps into the room, then stopped. "Alice, I know."

Seeing Steve was far different from what Alice had expected. Over the months she had played this scene in her mind a thousand times, and what she had envisioned was a nightmare. But now, the very sight of him filled her with a love she had almost forgotten in her panic. She did love this man, deeply, beyond all else. She suddenly knew that running had been foolish. She was glad he had caught her, though she was still terrified of the minutes that now lay ahead of them.

Alice tried to speak, but only sobs came forth from her swollen lips.

Steve moved to the bed and sat down. A suitcase separated them.

"Alice, I know why you are running, and I want to tell you that I understand. I want to tell you that there is no need to run. We belong together, no matter what."

Alice still couldn't believe that Steve knew the truth. He had to be talking about something else. No, he'd never understand if he knew the real truth.

"Don't say 'no matter what,' Steve. Some things are hard to live with."

Steve flipped the suitcase closed, opening the space between them. He moved to her, took her damp hands in his.

"We come first," Steve said. "You and me. That is

all we have right now, that is what is most valuable. If I lost you, I would be lost. We have to trust our love, trust in each other, no matter what. I'm an ex-convict, for crying out loud. Do you hate me for that? Would you leave me for that? No, you wouldn't. You love me, I know you do. I . . . Alice, what I'm trying to say is, children or no children, life without you is meaningless for me. You are the most important thing in my life, now and forever."

It took a few moments for his words to sink in. Alice heard them, yet did not immediately believe she was hearing them. Her dark fantasies were still too overwhelming. But then the words did begin to make sense. She heard them with both her heart and mind. And then she felt months of anxiety, guilt and worry melting away, releasing her, freeing her.

Steve pulled her into his arms, and Alice clung hard to his firm body. She felt light, as if she had awakened from a terribly real dream to find that life was much, much better.

Through her tears, Alice began to laugh. Huge, heaving bursts of joy came forth as she ran her hands up his back and through his hair, kissed him over and over again on the cheeks, forehead, eyes, lips. He was solid, he was here and he loved her.

Steve cleared the bed and they stretched out, Alice cuddled securely at his side, her head resting over his pounding heart. And soon she drifted into a deep, contented sleep.

An hour later, she woke to find Steve searching her face with soulful eyes.

"What are you looking at?" she said weakly.

"My wife, my love, my future."

Alice smiled, kissed his cheek tenderly, then lowered her head to his shoulder. "I don't know what to say or do."

Steve stroked her hair. "We've both been through hell. There's only one thing left to do."

"What?"

"It's something we should have done four months ago, but were denied."

"Tell me, what?"

"Have us a honeymoon we'll never forget."

"Oh, Steve!"

And, reunited at last, Steve and Alice Frame embraced.

Chapter Six
Sweet Endings

Robert had broken his usual tradition and had not taken Lenore out to an elegant or expensive restaurant. They now shared an intimate and private candlelit table for two at a small French restaurant that was tucked away on one of Bay City's side streets.

Outside, the April night was cool, refreshing, full of the promise of springtime. Inside, both of them were excited but tentative.

All week long, Lenore had anticipated this evening, and day by day she had done little things to prepare. She had purchased a new dress with shoes to match. She had had her hair trimmed and waved. Though she didn't need it, she had bought new makeup, had had her nails done, and had even sat through a waxing of her legs. Tonight, she felt and looked better than she ever had in her life.

"Have I told you that you look lovely?" Robert asked, taking a sip of his wine.

"No, you haven't," Lenore said. "You told me I looked breathtaking and gorgeous, but not lovely. Thank you."

Robert chuckled and shook his head.

They sat in silence for many moments, looking into each other's eyes.

"What did you order?" Robert asked.

"The same as you."

"Oh," he said. "And what did I order?"

"The same as me," Lenore said with a wide smile.

"Oh, *that*," Robert said. He unfolded his napkin and placed it across his thigh, raised his wine glass, sipped, replaced it on the table, smiled at Lenore and sighed.

Lenore felt as if her heartbeats would shake the wine right out of their glasses. She suspected what the occasion was and could barely control her whirling mind. How would it happen? When would he say those words? How would she react? What if he asked her when she had a mouthful of lemon sole?

And what was wrong with Robert?

Usually totally in control, usually taking charge and full of conversation and observations, Robert was having trouble. He was collapsing into himself, nervous, with beads of perspiration dotting his brow.

Was he having doubts?

No, Lenore decided. She knew him and loved him and was certain that Robert returned it all hundredfold. Still, she didn't know how much longer she could wait without screaming.

Dinner arrived.

"This looks delicious," Robert said. And he focused all his attention on the fish before him.

Lenore was too excited to eat. She picked, tried to indulge Robert in any kind of conversation. He'd grunt, he'd fake a laugh, he'd wipe his hands about fifty times. He went to the men's room three times.

Lenore was beginning to feel the first pricklings of

anger. She had agonized for weeks about her feelings toward Robert, examining herself from every possible angle, exposing all her doubts, playing antagonist on every point. The end result was that, yes, she loved this man dearly and, yes, she would be more than willing and ready to marry him. They had talked about marriage, had coyly mentioned the advantages of married life, expressing little domestic things they liked about each other. All these things Lenore had to go through before the question of being ready became a thing of the past.

And now she was not receiving her reward. Robert was withholding that all-valuable question.

Maybe if I kicked him under the table, she thought. *No. Maybe I should ask him! Boy, wouldn't that shock him!*

Lenore did nothing but wait.

Their dinner plates were taken away.

By the time dessert arrived, Lenore was near panic. She fidgeted in her chair, cleared her throat repeatedly, smiled purposely at Robert to egg him onward every time he looked at her.

A few times, Robert sat upright and leaned toward her. The words were written all over his face but nothing came out of his mouth.

When Robert took the last bite of his pastry, Lenore leaned forward.

"I love you," she said.

With that, she had pushed the right button.

Robert sighed heavily. His hand shot inside his jacket pocket. He lowered his hand to his lap. With his other hand, he gently grasped her left hand and pulled it toward him. He isolated her third finger, raised it, and brought his other hand to hers. He slipped on her finger a diamond ring so large that

Lenore gasped. Her eyes filled with tears, which ran uninhibitedly down her powdered cheeks.

Robert met her eyes and smiled with raised eyebrows.

Lenore, in a quiet, whispery voice, said, "Yes."

Rachel was doing something she hadn't done in years: she was spending the night at her mother's house.

Upstairs and alone in bed, her subdued evening with Ada, Gil and Jamie behind her, Rachel turned her face into the pillow and wept.

Nothing and no one was waiting ahead for her. After the scene with Steve in his office, she had wondered what made her the kind of woman she was. She felt confused, definitely in the wrong and desperate.

But, characteristically, she did not dwell on self-criticism for long. Instead, she fell into a deep abyss of self-pity. Inside, she felt hollow, rejected, abused by the world in general. She felt unloved, without hope, misunderstood.

Rachel's bag of cruel tricks was empty for the first time in her life.

The next morning, Rachel padded down to the kitchen in slippers and robe. It felt good and comfortable not to immediately shower and primp for the challenges of the day. Ada was already brewing a pot of coffee. Rachel slumped in a chair and played with the salt shaker.

"You're getting salt all over the table," Ada said.

"Sue me."

"I'll spank you, I swear I will. And you could use it, too, I might add."

Rachel smiled at her and put the salt shaker aside.

"Coffee?" Ada asked.

"Five cups, if you don't mind."

Ada poured Rachel a mug and set it before her. Rachel took her coffee black. She sipped it, then held the mug in both hands. The slight pain of the heat felt good.

Ada poured herself a cup and joined Rachel at the table.

"Want to talk about it?"

"About what?"

"About what has ruined your life and reduced you to a sad-eyed mope."

Rachel shrugged.

"Was it Steve?"

"Of course it was Steve, he . . ." Rachel stopped and rubbed her nose. "No, it was me."

"Rachel, you're a powerful woman, only you don't know it. Inside you is the power to make yourself happy, if you really want to."

"Well, that's stupid. Of course I want to."

"No, you don't. You want to steal someone else's happiness. Doing that, all you end up with is nothing."

Rachel didn't object. Her mother had always been perceptive enough to hit the nail right on the head. That's why Rachel needed her.

"What do I want from life, Mom?" Rachel said.

"What do you want for your own life?" Ada said. "A man? A family? A business? A hobby?"

Rachel refused to cry. She choked down tears and, to cover herself, rose to refill her coffee mug.

"Karate?" Ada said.

Rachel laughed. "I guess I'm temporarily depressed," she said.

"I guess so. Come here, sit down. I have something to tell you."

"I'm really not in the mood for a lecture," Rachel said.

"No lectures, I promise," Ada said. "This is something guaranteed to cheer you up."

"It'll have to be a miracle to do that."

"It is, it is."

Rachel sat back in her chair and studied her mother. Ada was absolutely glowing, beaming. A smile spread across her mother's kind face the likes of which Rachel had never seen before. Ada began fussing with her robe, smoothing it out, buttoning the top button. The whole process made Rachel smile.

"Well, out with it. What's up?" Rachel said.

"The best possible news," Ada said. She patted her belly. "I'm going to have a baby, Rachel. I'm pregnant, three months' worth. We waited until we were sure—and until Gil got over his shock. What do you think, huh?"

"I don't believe it!"

Ada nodded and nodded. "Yes, yes, it's true!"

"It's . . . it's incredible!"

"Yes, yes!"

Rachel rose and hugged her mother, who patted Rachel all over her back in her excitement. Mother and daughter were in tears.

Soon they settled down and Rachel took her seat.

"A baby," Rachel said. "A half-sister for me to share my toys with."

"Who would have thought?" Ada said. "But, heck, I'm still young enough, and goodness knows Gil's still got a lot of spunk left." She blushed.

"I couldn't be happier for you, Mom," Rachel said.

"Thank you, honey. That means more to me than I could say."

Later, in the privacy of the shower, Rachel confronted feelings she had subdued down in the kitchen. She stood still under the gushing spray and tried to sort out the confusion of her churning emotions.

With her mother suddenly pregnant with new life, Rachel suddenly felt lifeless. And she felt old. Age was something she had rarely applied to herself. She had always been confident that she appeared youthful, with youthful traits and attractiveness. But now she was forced to confront the passage of time, of time gone by, time wasted, of so little time ahead. And the last thing she needed was a little sister or brother to remind her.

She wasn't even sure that she could cope with her mother's baby. Rachel felt more like a mother than a sibling, and that is what the child would be, a sibling. Rachel knew she'd have gray hair before she could speak to her sister on any intelligent level at all.

She shampooed her hair, scrubbing furiously, refusing to confront these depressing feelings. *I still have my own life to live*, she thought. *I have to somehow rebound from this pit I'm in, this horrible, depressing sense of failure. I have to find my own hope for the future.*

More than anything, Rachel wished there was someone she could talk to, someone who would understand. Mothers were one thing, but she needed to talk with someone who saw her as an adult woman, not a child, not a sister, not a sibling.

As she was toweling off, admiring herself in the steamy mirror, she suddenly realized that there was such a person.

There was Mac Cory.

Over the past month and a half, he had called frequently. She had even gone out with him for dinner, to the movies, for a stroll through an art museum, which she found surprisingly fascinating. But until now, she had treated their relationship lightly.

Yes, she decided, she could talk to Mac. He was open, he was kind and even if he was a little too doting and excessive, he was always ready to listen and to be sympathetic. And he was not bad-looking, either. Yes, she was even proud to be seen with him.

All right, she said to herself. *Time to take charge. I know when I'm down, and I am as down as I've ever been. I'm getting nowhere on my own, and it is time to recognize the one friend I do have.*

She took one last look in the mirror. And I'm not old. In fact, to Mac I must look like quite a spring chicken.

After dressing, she phoned him immediately.

Lenore and Robert decided to have the most extravagant wedding possible. Over the next three months, they spent some of their best times together planning, organizing and generally getting excited about the wedding.

And they didn't ignore each other, either. They treated themselves lavishly, nurturing their romance and providing a firm and exciting foundation on which to build their future together.

Lenore no longer doubted Robert or her love for him. For her, this was a miraculous new beginning, a chance she thought she would never have again.

Janet Williams was to be her maid of honor, a choice that she and Robert thought both appropriate and funny. Lenore spent many happy hours with Janet, visiting shops, fabric centers and tailors, piecing together an original wedding gown that would become the most beautiful ever created. They decided on color schemes of greens and light-yellows for the bride's maids, ribbons, floral arrangements and place settings.

The society columns ate up the story of the architect and the widow, of the scandal of her past and her present triumph of snaring a royal and rich knight. Everyone loves gossip and dirt, but everyone also loves a happy ending.

On a sunny June third at ten o'clock in the morning, Lenore Curtin married Robert Delaney in the towering St. Michael's Cathedral in Bay City.

The reception at the Knollcrest Golf and Country Club was attended by two hundred fifty guests. A full, tuxedoed orchestra played songs from the forties, a staff of sixty white-clad waiters served filet mignon, lobster tails and a wide array of appetizers, finger food and delicacies. A golden fountain with pink champagne bubbled near a wide picture window overlooking the lush, green ninth fairway.

Lenore and Robert, glowing and kissing at every request, made the rounds, greeting and thanking their fond friends and guests.

Robert escorted her toward a voluptuous blonde with the greenest eyes Lenore had ever seen. She wore a pink satin gown that hugged her like a second skin. As they approached, the woman smiled widely, showing off a handsome set of cheekbones that Lenore envied.

"Lenore," Robert said, "I'd like you to meet Carol Lamonte. She's a fellow architect in my office, and a good one too."

"How do you do," both women said at the same time.

"I'm sorry I missed you when you stopped by the office," Carol said. "I've been wanting to meet you. Bob has talked about no one else for, oh, months."

Lenore smiled tightly. Did Carol mean to insinuate that Bob had talked about someone else before that? *No*, Lenore thought, *I must be mistaken.*

"I enjoyed the wedding tremendously," Carol went on. "But soon the honeymoon will be over and it will be back to work as usual. Right, Bobbie?"

Robert blinked several times and tried a smile of his own. It was false.

Yes, Lenore knew, this woman was, for some reason, being deliberately antagonistic. Why on earth? Lenore had never met her before.

"Nice meeting you, Miss Lamonte. Come on, Robert, guests await."

Carol smiled, and Lenore gratefully left her. As they talked with someone at the next table, Lenore heard Carol behind her loudly complaining to a waiter about the toughness of the filet. What was wrong with that woman?

Forget her, Lenore thought. *Nothing is going to spoil this day for me, nothing.*

A few hours later, with flashbulbs popping, with Wally waving at Janet's side, with Lenore in a stylish white summer suit and Robert in a rakish tan linen suit, the happy couple posed at the top of the staircase, then were whisked off via a limousine toward a six-week European honeymoon.

Their lives together had begun, carrying them atop a wave of love and excitement Lenore thought would never end.

Chapter Seven
Love and Fire

Three weeks later, summer had officially arrived in all its beautiful, balmy and sun-drenched glory. At this time of year, Bay City's population seemed to triple, because everyone took to the streets, the parks and the pools to lift faces to the golden sky and to parade the very best of hot-weather wardrobes.

And Rachel was no exception. *Summer belongs to me*, she thought. *No one looks better in light cottons and pressed linens than I do*. Two walk-in closets were full of her finery: colorful custom-made dresses, skirts, blouses, suits and slinky frocks from top designers the world over. And shoes, at least a hundred pair, sculpted to slip over her slender feet and showcase the best ankles in Bay City.

Rachel lifted a foot to the mirror. "Mirror, mirror on the wall, who has the prettiest ankles of them all?" She giggled at herself and did a little time-step until the foolishness of it all made her blush.

God, I am happy, she thought.

The phone rang beside her queen-sized bed. She leaped and sprawled full length, rolled over and brought the receiver to her ear.

"Good morning!" she said.

"You knew it was me, didn't you?" Mac said from the other end.

"Your ring has a certain something about it," Rachel said.

"Sexy," he said. "I dial a very sexy phone."

"Mac?" Rachel said. "I've got great ankles, don't you think?"

"They should be in the Louvre."

"Oh, Mac! Then what would I walk on?"

Mac laughed. "You could walk on cloud nine. Like me."

"I am."

"Do you know what time it is?"

Rachel rolled her eyes to the bedside clock. "Eight-fifteen in the glorious morning."

"Will you make it by nine-thirty?"

"Aren't I always on time?"

"Yes," he said. "I can always count on you to be precisely ten minutes late."

"I like to know you're there when I walk into a room."

"I'll always be there for you, Rachel."

Rachel sighed. "This line is getting awfully mushy."

"Okay, okay. See you at nine-thirty then."

"Then."

Rachel gently replaced the receiver..

Rachel, she said to herself. *What is happening to you?*

That is exactly the question that all of Bay City was

asking. Increasingly, day by day, over the past three weeks, Rachel had been evolving into an apparently different person. Bay City saw it, yet no one could yet truly believe that this spiteful, scheming, scandalous woman could possibly change. But the evidence was there for everyone to see, written all over Rachel's beautiful face.

It was love. From the second she had decided to phone Mac three weeks ago, the dark cloud hovering over her life had begun to dissipate. Mac's arm became a life preserver, a rock, a security blanket. She couldn't do without it for long. And when she had discovered that attached to that arm was a man like none other in the entire world, Rachel began to see the world through different eyes. She began to see a bright future.

Rachel tightened the belt on a full-skirted turquoise cotton dress, then paused. Dark doubts suddenly swept through her mind, sending a wave of uncomfortable hotness up her back and chest.

I don't deserve this, she thought. *I don't really deserve to be this happy. Something is bound to go wrong. Something horrible. It always does. It is only a matter of when.*

She sat on the edge of her bed, near tears. Her heel touched something hard. Immediately, she knew what it was. She reached down under the bed and brought up a framed photograph of Steve. She had always kept it there, to stare at and dream at during late nights when sleep eluded her troubled mind. Steve's handsome features and penetrating eyes had deeply affected her, had fired feelings of regret, loss, deep love, anger and revenge.

She stared back into his eyes once again. Nothing.

You can now order previous titles of *Soaps & Serials*™ Books by mail!

Just complete the order form, detach, and send together with your check or money order payable to:

Soaps & Serials™
120 Brighton Road, Box 5201
Clifton, NJ 07015-5201

- -

Please <u>circle</u> the book #'s you wish to order:

The Young and The Restless	1	2	3	4	5	6
Days of Our Lives......	1	2	3	4	5	6
Guiding Light..........	1	2	3	4	5	6
Another World.........	1	2	3	4	5	6
As The World Turns....	1	2	3	4	5	6
Dallas™.................	1	2	3	4	5	6
Knots Landing™	1	2	3	4	5	6
Capitol™................	1	2	3	4	NOT AVAILABLE	

Each book is $2.50 ($3.25 in Canada).

Total number of books
circled _____ × price above = $ _____ .

Sales tax (CT and NY residents only) $ _____ .

Shipping and Handling $ _____ .95

Total payment enclosed $ _____ .
(check or money orders only)

Name _____

Address _____ Apt# ____

City _____

State _____ Zip _____

Telephone (_____) _____
Area code   AW6

She felt nothing. It was as if Steve was merely part of a distant past, almost as if he had been involved in another woman's life and not Rachel's. Such was the effect that Mac Cory had on her life.

Luck, Rachel said to herself. *Blind luck.*

She was referring to Mac's arrival in her life. She felt she had lucked into the right man at exactly the right time. Why such wonderful good luck had come to her, she couldn't figure out. She couldn't figure out whether she deserved it, but there he was nonetheless. Her rich, spunky, fearless fifty-seven-year-old white knight. *No, no*, Rachel thought. *He's not a white knight. He's Superman. He's got x-ray vision. He can see right through me.*

Mac openly admitted to Rachel that for him it had been love at first sight. He told her frankly that he knew she was hurting badly inside, and that was one of the things that drew him to her. He desired to help her, to heal her. But he also loved her tough emotional exterior, he'd said. "Just like me," he'd said.

Rachel slid Steve's picture back under the bed. "Bye-bye."

She discovered a tear on her cheek and gently brushed it away. The tear was not for Steve, she knew. It was for Mac. For the many times he'd allowed her to cry on his shoulder. For the times he'd told her point-blank to grow up. For the times he dove into her soul and expressed things she had never heard before in her life, things she needed to hear badly, such as: "Rachel, you've had a tough life. It's time for you to forgive yourself."

The phone rang.

Rachel answered. "Hello?"

"Guess where I am?"

"Mac?" Rachel giggled. "The moon?"

"Nope," Mac said. "Guess again. I'll give you a hint. Look at the clock."

Rachel looked. "Oh, no! How'd it get so late? You're already at my mother's?"

"Bingo."

"I'm gone."

Rachel hung up, blew a kiss to herself in the mirror and rushed out of the room.

As Rachel walked up to her mother's front door, she wondered what the occasion was. Ada had never invited her or anyone over for brunch. It wasn't her style. Something must be up.

Without knocking, Rachel walked through the door. Gales of laughter greeted her from the living room. Mac had probably been telling one of his stories, and both Ada and Gil were cracking up.

Rachel grinned warmly. From the very first time she had introduced Mac to her mother and stepfather, they'd hit it off. Quickly, Mac had become a friend of the family. Family, Rachel thought. When was the last time she felt a solid sense of family?

The first person to greet Rachel was her son, Jamie.

"Mom! Mom!" Jamie said, storming up to her. "Hi!"

"Hi, honey." She kissed him on the cheek. He was looking more like Steve every day. But still, there was some Rachel in his eyes, his cheekbones. If she could only resolve her feelings about Jamie, as she had resolved them about Mac, she could finally feel whole.

"You should have heard the story Mac just told," Jamie said. "What a riot. All about some polar bear up in Alaska by the oil line."

Rachel laughed. "I've heard that one a million times."

Jamie just stood there anxiously.

"What's up? What's the matter?"

"Oh, nothing," he said. "It's just that, well, Grandma said I have to stick around because I never see you and you never see me and everything."

"I'm seeing you now," Rachel said. "So what's the problem?"

"Well, see, Billy's got this great new game. He just called. But Grandma said I couldn't go over."

"Oh," Rachel said, thinking. "How about if you go over for a little while, then come back? That way you can see Billy and me."

"Yeah!"

"Rachel?" Ada, more than five months pregnant, was waddling toward her daughter.

"Hi, fatso," Rachel said, hugging her mom.

"Was that Jamie I just saw run out the door?"

"Yes. I told him he could go, for a little while."

Ada shook her head, then patted her belly. "You'll never catch me spoiling my kid like that."

An inexplicable tightness grabbed Rachel's throat. She tried to smile through it. Her mother's pregnancy was something that still troubled her deeply. But why? Rachel couldn't put her finger on it.

Mac came up and interrupted her thoughts with a long kiss on her cheek. As he did so, he whispered in her ear. "Relax, honey. Everything will be fine."

God, this man knew her inside and out. She squeezed his arm.

Mac held her at arm's length. "Absolutely lovely."

Ada shook her head and looked at her daughter's slim figure, then her own balloon body. "I feel like Santa Claus next to her."

Gil hugged Ada. "Santa never delivered a present like the one you will."

"Okay, everybody," Mac said. "Into the living room."

Something's going to happen, Rachel thought. Something is definitely going on.

Ada, Gil and Mac hurried into the living room and sat down. *They're like children*, Rachel thought, shaking her head and smiling. Excitement was written all over their faces. Rachel sat down beside Mac and everyone fell silent.

"Okay," Rachel finally said, "what's going on?"

"Why, what on earth do you mean?" Ada said, grinning from ear to ear.

Mac leaned toward Ada. "You can't fool Rachel for long," he said.

"Is someone going to tell me?" Rachel's curiosity was beginning to turn fearful.

"Help me up, Gil," Ada said. "Come on, I want to show you the kitchen."

"Oh, boy," Gil said. "What a treat."

They left.

"Why do they have to leave us alone?" Rachel said to Mac. Then she stopped, because Mac's face was beaming like the summer sun. He looked ten years younger and was flushed like a boy on his first date.

"What *is* going on?" Rachel said, smiling widely.

Mac touched his forehead. "I'm psychic," he said.

Rachel laughed.

"No, no, really. I can see the future. I can see far into the future."

Rachel was too impatient to play one of Mac's little games. She laid a hand on his arm. "Mac, please."

Mac lowered his eyes to hers. "I love you, Rachel."

"I know," she said. "I love you, too. More and differently than I've ever loved anyone before."

Rachel heard a creak behind her. She spun in her seat in time to see Ada quickly close the kitchen door. She turned back to Mac. "They're peeking! They're listening! Will someone please tell me . . . Oh!"

In Mac's hand was the biggest diamond ring she had seen in her entire life.

"I told you I could see the future," Mac said. "And what I saw, for years and years, was you and me. Together. Happy. Growing. Loving. So I figured, what the heck, why wait? Will you marry me, Rachel?"

In a split second, a thousand feelings and thoughts flew through her mind. Her tortured history with Steve, winning him, losing him, tricking him, having him, loving him, hating him. But never had she felt for Steve what she felt for Mac. She never had to win Mac, or trick him, or manipulate him, or seduce him. Mac was just always there, waiting with open arms and an open heart. And it left Rachel free to be herself, the good and bad, the ugly and giving—she could throw it all in front of Mac and he always stood by her, loved her, understood her and gave her what she needed.

Then she thought, *This will show them all, Steve and Bay City and all of them. It will show them I'm not a loser, that I deserve a good man like Mac. That I . . . No, wait. What am I thinking?* In Rachel's heart of hearts she knew that, at last, she wasn't doing something for anyone else but herself. This was her choice, her life; she had Mac and she didn't have to prove anything to anyone. At last, she had a life of her own.

Rachel swallowed. "Yes, Mac. Oh, yes!"

Before Rachel and Mac could embrace, Ada and Gil came storming out of the kitchen, cheering and clapping.

Rachel, through her tears and laughter, pressed into Mac's arms and kissed him deeply. Then he lifted her left hand and slid on the pear-shaped diamond. It nearly reached her knuckle. She held it up to the light, turning it this way and that, then took Mac's chin in her hand.

"Mac, the ring is gorgeous. But I wouldn't care if it was made of tin. The great gift you've given me is you."

"Well," Mac said, "I can always take the ring back."

She balled her fist. "Just try it!"

"Congratulations," both Ada and Gil said, exchanging hugs all around.

"So, when's the date?" Ada said.

"Good question," Mac said. "What do you think, Rachel?"

The fact was that Rachel couldn't think at all. "I . . . well . . . gee."

"I was thinking that maybe we could elope," Mac said. "Just disappear, quick as a flash."

"I don't know about that," Rachel said. "I'd kind of like to enjoy being engaged for a little while at least."

"The Fourth of July is coming up in about two weeks," Ada said. "Why not start your life off with a bang! Fireworks! Celebration! You couldn't ask for a better send-off!"

"Unless you'd like a big wedding," Mac said.

"No, I don't think so," Rachel said. The thorn still in her side was that most people in town treated her coolly. She didn't want to run the risk of no one showing up at her wedding.

Mac, as usual, knew exactly what she was thinking. "Let's keep it small, intimate, romantic. Courthouse marriage, family only, and fly off on a honeymoon through the fireworks."

Rachel hugged him. "Perfect."

Gil rubbed his hands together. "Well, now that that's settled, where's brunch?"

Ada looked at him. "What brunch?"

"Are you out of your mind!"

People in the restaurant turned in their seats.

"Shhh," Mac said.

"Are you crazy?" Iris said.

Mac didn't answer. Frankly, he was afraid to. He felt that his daughter was seriously close to breaking down.

Father and daughter had made this luncheon date a few days ago. At that time, Mac had Rachel's engagement ring but hadn't decided when to ask her to marry him. Coincidentally, he'd asked her mere hours ago. Now he had sprung the news on Iris, and the suddenness of it shocked Iris to the core.

"I can't believe you're serious," Iris said. "Think about what you're doing."

"I have."

"Mac, you're old enough to be her father."

"Which makes me old enough to be her husband. I love her, Iris. Can't help myself. She loves me, too."

Iris was visibly shaking. "She loves your money, Mac. Believe me, I know Rachel better than you do. Ask anyone in this town."

Go easy, Mac thought. Something was happening

here that he didn't quite understand. He never had fully understood his daughter, but he did know that she had recently recovered from a serious breakdown and the news he had just given her seemed like the last thing in the world Iris wanted to hear—and the last thing she ever expected.

"It's just ridiculous, that's all," Iris said, groping for words. "She's not good enough for you. She's not good for anyone. Every man she's ever had was ruined by her. She's a life wrecker, that's what she is. She's . . . she's . . ."

Don't cry, Iris thought. *Don't let him see you cry. Don't ask for pity, no. But this is the wildest and craziest and most crushing thing that could have happened. Rachel! Of all the women Mac could have chosen. That scheming, selfish . . . Oh, I'll bet Rachel is laughing her head off right now.*

Iris took a sip of water. She couldn't help but take the whole shocking thing personally. Rachel had always loved sticking it to Iris, and she had certainly found the perfect way to do it this time. *Control, must control myself. Have to talk reason to Mac. Have to do my best.*

Iris's mind flashed back to hers and Mac's brunch in this very restaurant when he'd first come back from New York. For a few brief and hopeful moments, they were truly father and daughter. Then, Iris had felt that her world was finally changing. She desperately wanted Mac's love, the love only a father could give her, the love she never had and never really sought. Well, she was seeking it then and she was seeking it now—needed it now, needed it badly. And now Rachel had taken it all away.

Iris was far too upset to realize the essence of what she was feeling. Jealousy. In her complex emotional state, Iris saw Rachel as competition, as if Mac had only one kind of love to give and he was now pledging it to Rachel. Iris couldn't see through the fog of her emotional rage to the love that was clearly evident on Mac's kind face. Instead, she felt betrayed. She felt she had bared her soul and love to her father and he had cruelly cast it aside in favor of a hussy who hung all over him.

No one, she thought, *does this to Iris Carrington and gets away with it.*

Thankfully, Iris felt her wild and confusing anger simmering down. She had lost a battle, but not the war. Oh, no. Now she had to plan. She needed a course of action.

"You're really going to go through with this?" Iris said.

Mac was frightened by what he saw in his daughter's eyes. It was a fire he had never seen before. A cold, hard look that he hoped to God wasn't hate. There was no doubt in his mind at all about Rachel and his love for her or hers for him. His only worry now was Iris's well-being. She was mixed up, confused somehow, threatened for some reason. He desperately wanted to help her but he knew that, in the space of a few minutes, she had completely shut him out and turned against him. What could he do?

"I love Rachel, Iris," Mac said. "I've never been happier. She needs me and she loves me, too."

"She's tricking you," Iris said. "You're an old fool not to see it."

"Listen, Iris," Mac said. "Why don't we go somewhere this afternoon? Huh? Just the two of us. Sailing, maybe. Out into the bay. The day is too gorgeous to waste."

Iris slowly shook her head. "Too late, Mac. You can't bribe me. You're worried so much about wasting this day; why not stop to think that maybe you're wasting the rest of your life with her."

Mac had heard just about all he could take. "You're acting like a spoiled brat." As soon as he'd said it, he knew it was the wrong thing to say.

Iris slapped her napkin down with a loud smack. She leaned across the table, peering over a long finger she was pointing at Mac's face. "You're taking sides against your own daughter, and I don't like it. You're making a big mistake and you can't be adult enough to listen to reason. Your mind is fuzzy with infatuation for a pretty, scheming face, and you're making a fool of yourself. I'm telling you, the woman you are going to marry would like nothing better in this world than to destroy me."

The people in the restaurant had fallen virtually silent, watching the drama before them unfold. A young man on the other side of the room took a reporter's pad from his breast pocket and began scribbling furiously.

"Iris, please. Sit down," Mac said. He was stunned. For the first time, he was seeing the full tragedy of his daughter, the bottled-up emotions and fears and hatreds that had risen to crush her once and could very soon do so again. His heart went out to her, and he cursed himself for not knowing any better than to spring this announcement on her so suddenly. Why hadn't he had a talk with her? Why hadn't he *thought*?

"I will not sit down!" Iris boomed. "Mark my

words, Mac, I'm going to show you what kind of woman you think you're going to marry."

Mac rose. "Come on, let's talk. This is no place—"

"It's exactly the place!" Iris said, including the whole room. "They all know what Rachel is. But only you, Mac, only you know what you're doing to your own daughter. I promise you, I won't stop until I make certain that Rachel gets just what she deserves."

Iris turned on her heels and stormed out of the restaurant. Mac reached into his wallet, dropped a hundred-dollar bill on the table and walked swiftly after her. When he stepped outside, Iris was gone.

Over the next two weeks, Mac tried many times to reach Iris but failed. A dark cloud had suddenly swept in over his idyllic life, and no one felt it more than Rachel.

"You know she has problems, Mac," Rachel said. "She'll get over it, you'll see."

"I hope so."

She tweaked his cheek. "Oh, stop it now. Nothing is your fault. You can't live her life for her, Mac. She makes her own choices. The only trouble is that her emotions get in the way. It happens to all of us from time to time. She loves you, Mac. Give her time."

Mac hugged her. "I guess you're right."

Two days later, the Fourth of July arrived. The day began drizzly and overcast, but by wedding time at noon, the sun broke free and warmed the wet streets.

Mac and Rachel managed to forget their problems and were caught up in the excitement of their life together. Mac, Rachel noted, was acting just like a schoolboy, flushing and shy and eager. She couldn't stop staring at him.

The wedding was just as they had decided, a simple affair at the Bay City courthouse. Rachel wore a cream-colored dress, pearls and white gloves, with a selection of colorful flowers in her hands. Mac wore a tuxedo. Gil and Ada and Jamie were there, as well as a few other close friends. Mac had invited Iris, of course, but, of course, she was not there. Mac kept peering over his shoulder all the same.

After the "I wills" were said and the rings were exchanged and the kiss was planted, Mac let loose with a loud whoop and twirled Rachel in his arms to the astonishment and delight of all.

Accepting handshakes and hugs, dodging rice, the newlyweds ran out of the courthouse and slid happily into the limousine waiting to take them to the airport.

Inside, they kissed again.

"Oh, this is the happiest day of my life!" Rachel said.

"And the beginning of a new life for both of us," Mac said.

As the limo began slowly to pull away from the curb, Mac turned toward the rear to wave. That's when he saw Iris. Through the blue-gray tinted glass the day looked gloomy, and there, standing on the other side of the square, was Iris. At that moment, she turned and disappeared around a corner.

Mac's face grew tight. He was grateful that Rachel didn't know the full truth about Iris's threats. He was relieved that he'd intercepted Iris's horrible letters to Rachel. Mac had even managed to keep the newspapers out of Rachel's hands—the society page was splashed with information, slander and photographs of what had happened in the restaurant with Iris. The articles did not present Rachel in a kind light, to say the least.

"We're off!" Rachel said.

Mac settled back and let calm wash over him. He wasn't going to allow anything to ruin this day or the honeymoon for either him or Rachel. London, Paris, then Egypt and Greece. Six weeks of paradise with his lovely wife. Six glorious weeks that he deserved after a lifetime of hard work. Six weeks for Iris to, he hoped, see the light.

"Well, my queen," Mac said. "It's more than an hour to the airport. What would you like? A drink? A sandwich? An emerald necklace? Some television?"

"A *what?*"

Mac handed her a long, white satin box. "For the new Mrs. Cory. From her honorable and most loving slave."

Rachel opened the box. There lay a necklace of seven pure African emeralds encased in fragile gold settings. "Oh, Mac! This is the most gorgeous necklace I've ever seen in my life!"

"I agree," Mac said. "In fact, I almost bought one for myself."

Silently, Rachel reached into her small purse and handed Mac a small black box. "For you," she said.

It was a solid-gold money clip in the shape of a key.

"It's the key to my heart, Mac," Rachel said. "No matter what happens, no matter what is up ahead for us, that key will always work. I love you, Mac."

She kissed him. He returned the kiss vigorously, wetting it with a single tear.

Chapter Eight
Guilty Parties

Lenore felt as if she were perched on top of a cloud. She stood on the large deck of Robert's—and her own—breathtaking cliff-side home. From above, the hot August sun fell full on her face and a gentle breeze tossed her long hair. She grasped the railing and peered down the cliff face, which plunged to the tree line far below and swept outward into the valley toward Bay City.

The honeymoon was nearly a month over, and her and Robert's life together had begun. But not until today did Lenore really and truly feel their lives come together. It should have been one of the happiest days of her life. It wasn't turning out that way.

"You okay out there?" Robert called from within the house.

"I'm fine," Lenore called back.

"Don't get too close to the edge."

"All right." *He's treating me like a child,* she thought. *No, no, I'm just grouchy, that's all.*

She heard Robert barking orders to the moving

men. The men moving Lenore's things. The things she cherished, loved, cared for. She couldn't bear to watch those burly men handle them.

She looked back down into the valley, trying to spot the wonderful house that she and Wally had called home for so many years. The house that had been a very real part of their family. The house that was now gone, sold to strangers, out of her life.

Is it really true I'll never be going back to that house? she wondered. *Yes, it's true.*

Naturally, she and Robert couldn't live in separate houses. Robert had pleaded a very logical argument for Lenore's moving into his. It was larger. It was newer. It was more private. And it had cost Robert hundreds of thousands to design and build into the cliff.

Lenore had finally agreed. But she had wanted desperately to keep her house, perhaps rent it. She had liked knowing that her special place was there, was hers, a part of her world.

Robert had talked her out of that idea, too. The tax burden would be ridiculous, he'd said. The maintenance. Besides, he'd said, the market had peaked out and, he explained, Lenore would never get as much money for the house later as she would now. All very practical.

"Merging two lives," Robert had said, "involves some sacrifices. But we do them willingly for the promise of greater things with the one we love."

So Lenore's and Wally's home was put on the market and sold. Now the question remained how to fit all of Lenore's possessions into Robert's house.

"I think we'll have to put some things in storage," Robert had said. "Perhaps auction them off at a later date—with some of my things, too, of course. But to tell you the truth, your furnishings were best suited for your house—heavy, wooden, cumbersome. They kind of clash around all the glass and Formica in my house, don't you think?"

Lenore didn't think so but, again, as Robert had said, some sacrifices had to be made.

So today was moving day. And Lenore didn't feel as if she was gaining all that much. In fact, she felt more like she was losing a great deal. She had to stop thinking like that, she decided. Stop being so possessive of her material things. *Robert's right, and no matter how I feel, I just can't ruin this new beginning for him.*

She wiped the tears from her big blue eyes, pinched her cheeks and took a huge breath of the clean air. *It is beautiful up here,* she thought. *So serene, a part of nature yet a part of the human world, too. I know I'll love this house, in time.*

Soon Robert came out to join her. He enclosed her with one arm and kissed her cheek.

"They're gone, at last," he said. "I don't think anything was damaged, either."

"That's good," Lenore said.

"I think that end table of yours, the one with the granite top, will go perfectly in the living room. Maybe your antique oval mirror, too. Touches of Lenore in the world of Robert." He stopped and studied her face. "You okay?"

She shrugged. "Oh, maybe a bit mellow."

"I know, I know," he said, tugging her shoulder. "The moving blues. Happens to everybody. It's not easy uprooting your life and moving up into the hills. Everything will be fine, believe me."

"I know it will."

"Hey, cheer up!"

She squeezed his arm. "I'm happy, honest. I was just thinking about my house down there, that's all."

"It's tough, I know. But it's money in the bank, Lenore. Your money. Money you can live on, enjoy life. That's what that house has given back to you."

"What do you mean?"

Robert moved a few steps away, then turned back. "I've been thinking. You have money, and I have money. And now that we're together, we really have it made, wouldn't you say?"

"I guess we do."

"So, I was thinking. Why go through all the day-to-day hassles and tensions of going to work every day? You're a smart, talented woman, Lenore. You don't need Frame Enterprises anymore. So quit! What do you think?"

Lenore was shocked. "Quit Frame? Why . . . what would I do?"

"Anything in the whole world you like."

"I don't think I could do that, Bob. The idea is absolutely scary. I like the job, I'm getting ahead."

"You're a slave to a corporation, and who needs that? I'm telling you, the best thing in the world for you is to quit. Make living your career. You know, house and home, Wally and me, doing the things you've always wanted to do."

"Here?" Lenore said, stunned. "You want me to spend all day, every day, here?"

"I thought you'd like the idea," Robert said, apparently hurt.

Lenore went to him. "Thank you, darling, for thinking about me. But I'm not cut out to be a housewife."

"Who said anything about being a housewife? Heck, we can afford maids, housekeepers, you name it."

"Again, Bob, what would I *do?*"

"Well, for one thing, you'd be here for me."

Lenore pulled away from him. "I can't believe you believe that. No, Bob, I'm not quitting. Sorry, but working is part of my life, part of the way I express myself."

"Okay, okay, don't get upset." Robert took her in his arms and rocked her for a few minutes. Then he spoke. "You're still adjusting to all this newness —being married, moving, selling your house. We'll talk about it later, after you're all settled in."

"I don't think I'll change my mind, Bob."

"We'll see."

That night, while Wally slept in his new bedroom and while Robert was brushing his teeth, Lenore lay in bed with the covers up to her chin. She was thinking about her and Robert's discussion and she realized that it had almost turned into a fight. There was a point there near the end when she had almost burst out and screamed at him.

Robert had only been looking out for her welfare. She couldn't blame him. She was still adjusting, adjusting to some things that Robert wasn't even aware of. Like having, loving, living with and trusting a man after so long. Yes, she must be more forgiving, less prone to reacting with her mixed-up emotions.

Tomorrow would be better. Then the next day even better. In time, she'd feel like a totally new woman.

Robert turned off the bathroom light and slid into bed.

"You okay?" he said.

"Sure," Lenore said. "You don't have to keep asking. I'm fine. I'm happy. And I'm very much in love with you."

They kissed.

"Tomorrow," he said, "do me a favor and wear that light-green dress of yours."

"The one with the yellow belt? Oh, Bob, I look fat in that thing."

"No, you don't. Wear it for me, okay?"

Lenore put her growing irritation aside. "Okay. Be glad to."

The next morning, frisky Janet Williams greeted Lenore by pulling her aside in the Frame Enterprises elevator and whispering, "Didn't you decide, just last week, that that dress makes you look fat? Did you lose weight or something?"

"Robert likes it," Lenore said.

"So, he's king of the hill already?" Janet saw something spark in Lenore's eyes. "Sorry, only kidding. All settled in?"

"Trying to. Robert's doing his best to keep me chipper, but it's strange being uprooted and transplanted."

"You mean his cave on the cliff is kinda weird, huh?"

Lenore giggled. "Kinda."

After work, Lenore rushed home and continued organizing her and Wally's things. She'd make this into her home, too, if it was the last thing she did. Wally helped by unpacking and arranging all his toys on the shelves in his room.

Robert came home with a dozen red roses.

"For the bride!" he announced with a bow.

"Oh, Bob, they're beautiful." Lenore ran off for her

favorite crystal vase and arranged the flowers on the dining-room table.

"And for you," Robert said to Wally, "a big surprise."

"What? What?" Wally said, jumping around.

"Nothing!" Robert said.

Wally's face dropped. "Oh."

Robert tickled Wally. "Only kidding, chum. Here you go, the latest robot tank. We need protection around here!"

"Oh, boy!" Wally snatched the toy and immediately dropped to the floor and began playing.

"That was nice of you," Lenore said to Robert. He was always so kind to Wally. It warmed Lenore's heart that he accepted her son so easily and happily.

Robert sniffed the air. "Hmmm. I don't smell anything."

"What do you mean?" Lenore said.

"What's for dinner?"

"I thought we'd eat out," Lenore said. "I've been so busy organizing myself."

"Oh, well," Robert said, "another dream of married life down the tubes."

Lenore went to him and gave him a big hug. "Don't you worry, as soon as I'm all settled in, you'll get the best dinners in the world waiting for you. Wally loves to cook, too. He's an expert on cookies."

"I don't know," Robert said. "Will it ever work out that way? Don't you think you're a little too busy to handle everything?"

"Definitely not," Lenore said. "I usually get home at least an hour before you close up shop. There's plenty of time."

"And what if you're late? Or I'm early? It's not going to work, darling."

Lenore crossed her arms protectively. She knew what was coming. "I can handle it, Bob."

"Seems like a big mess to me," he said. "You have to quit that job, Lenore. A house just isn't a home without a wife to take care of it."

"Bob, I told you that I don't mind being busy. I like it. You want dinner, you'll get dinner, every night. Starting in a few days, after I—"

"Settle in. I know," Robert said. "It's starting already."

"What's starting already?" Lenore said loudly.

Wally stopped his playing and looked up worriedly at his mom.

"The ridiculous demands on your time," Robert said. "We're a team now. A team has to work efficiently. We have responsibilities to each other and to our home. Eating out every night isn't my idea of a cozy family evening."

"Don't rush me!" Lenore shouted. "Give me a chance, will you? Can't you understand, even a little, what a huge change all this is for me?"

"Mom?" Wally said.

God, Lenore thought, *what's happening here?* She went to Wally and ruffled his hair. "It's okay. Wanna go for a ride?"

"Where are you going?" Robert said.

"Out for Chinese food. Be back in a few minutes." And without another word, Lenore and Wally left.

Not one day passed during the next week that Robert didn't again mention to Lenore that she should quit her job. More and more this became

Robert's obsession. Lenore would lay awake night after night, pondering the problem. Her first reaction was anger. She felt dominated, confused by Robert's possessiveness. It seemed to her that all he wanted was a home body for a wife. He wanted to steal her ambition, her drive, her excitement about her job and the outside world and turn her into his slave.

Then she thought, no. Bob couldn't be that despicable. She couldn't be that wrong. The man she had married she knew to be kind, giving, a doer. She had never seen him as angry or upset as he was now. It had to be her fault.

Some of their arguments were intense, and even the memory of them sent chills up Lenore's spine. Once, she had stormed into the bathroom, slamming the door, sitting in there doing nothing for more than an hour. Another time, she had picked up a glass and threatened to throw it at Robert, only to be stopped by Wally's frightened scream.

Yes, it was her fault. Even though she felt that she was right in defending her right to work, something was wrong with her. Somehow she was incapable of communicating with Robert. Lenore searched herself for faults, convinced that there must be something she could do to correct her flaws and make Robert happy. But nothing seemed to work.

Lenore confided in Janet, her closest friend. Janet told her it was all Robert's fault. Janet said she'd seen men like him before, men who are really nice and all that, but men who, for some reason, have to totally dominate their wives, tell them what to wear, tell them what to cook, keep them under one roof like a pet in a cage. Lenore agreed that Robert was somewhat like that, but Lenore thought that she was the one who made Robert that way.

And because of it all, Robert very quickly grew distant, staying later at work, silent during the evenings, unresponsive to her affection.

After many sad and tearful days, Lenore began to think that maybe she didn't deserve a husband. Maybe she was a plague to men. Maybe her hopes and dreams that life with Robert would be different were a sham. Maybe she was the cause of the horror that had turned out to be her first marriage. Maybe, indirectly or not, she was the real reason behind the blind rage that had driven Walter to an accidental murder.

Now, Wally stuck to his room in the evenings or begged to go over to a friend's house after dinner or for the night. Though Lenore left work early many nights to prepare wonderful meals for Robert, he sulked his way through them, the food not satisfying his total desire of what he thought a wife should be. And the more Lenore tried to cheer him up, the more she felt that, as a woman, she was a total failure.

Robert had designed his architectural offices himself. They were housed in a renovated turn-of-the-century New England-style house. He had chosen it for its relatively open location, just on the outskirts of Bay City.

Light was a very important factor in his business, and all his offices were flooded with light from the skylights and oversized windows he'd installed. Each of his draftsmen and architects had his or her own spacious office, for space was the next consideration after light.

Here and there on white pedestals were models of

some of the amazing structures he had designed and built. With tasteful, neutral tones of pale green, antique white and subtle woodwork, the entire effect was one of peace, creativity and success.

Midafternoon, three weeks after Robert had moved Lenore into his cliff-side mansion, he received a phone call at his office.

"Bob? It's me, Lenore."

"Hi."

"Listen, I'm really, really sorry, but I have to work late tonight. There's a huge marketing push I'm directly involved in. They've called an emergency meeting. Steve Frame told me personally that he expects me to be there. I've arranged for Wally to go home with his buddy Kevin. I'm really sorry. You'll be okay without me for a few hours?"

Robert sighed and rubbed his face. "The same old thing," he said.

"Please, Bob, not now, please. I've got too much on my mind."

"Something has to change, Lenore. And change now."

"Please don't worry. It'll all work out, honest. You'll see. I'll *make* it work out. I've got to run, okay? I love you, you know."

"I know. I'll just catch a burger or something —again. See ya." And Robert hung up.

He shook his head, rubbed his temples, then opened his eyes. Standing there in the doorway with her back to the light was Carol Lamonte, one of his assistant architects.

"Sorry, Bob, I didn't know you were on the phone," she said.

The old term "a knockout" sprang into Bob's mind. If any woman was a knockout, Carol Lamonte was. Natural, shimmering blond hair. Beautifully constructed face with lazy green eyes. A figure that tantalized from every angle. And flashy, come-hither clothes that you couldn't tear your eyes from.

"It's all right," Bob said.

Carol walked up close to the side of a slanted drafting table. Her musky-sweet perfume washed over Robert like a warm, welcome breeze.

"Troubles?" she asked.

"Who was the jerk who said that marriage was bliss?" Robert said, chuckling unconvincingly.

"It wasn't me," Carol said. "Want to talk about it?"

Carol had never been Robert's confidante, and the question both surprised and pleased him. He'd always thought of Carol as kind of distant—oh, she was aggressive sexually, but there was something about her personality that said "Knock before entering."

"No, thanks," Robert said. "I'll recoup in a minute."

"Tell you what. I just made some coffee. Let me get you a cup."

"That would be great," Robert said. He watched her go slowly out of his office, smoothing the sides of her dress as she went.

Every once in a while, Robert found himself strongly attracted to Carol, mostly because of her sultry looks. But he knew she was a dead end, a woman who could only lead to trouble, and certainly not the kind of woman he pictured as a wife.

No, he reminded himself, he didn't hire her for her looks. She was a sharp, inventive architect, with a refreshing perspective that often surprised him. She had come to Bay City from Los Angeles. She said she wanted the challenge of a growing community, one an architect could shape and watch hatch into a something cohesive and expressive. She'd received many offers, Robert recalled, some probably better than his, and he often wondered why she had chosen his firm. He suspected that she'd taken the job, in part, because of his reputation and, in part, because she was attracted to him—for Carol didn't keep secret what she felt.

She had once asked him out, but Robert's danger signals had flashed and he had said no. He suddenly remembered that his refusal came about two weeks before his wedding to Lenore. So that's why she was so testy at the reception. Old news.

Carol returned with the coffee.

"Thanks, I need this," Robert said, taking a sip.

"You're welcome," she said. "Next time it's your turn."

"Okay, I guess I'm ready for business. What do you have there, the Peterson plans?"

Carol unfolded a blueprint and a sheet of exterior elevations. "There's a problem here on the second-floor front." She moved closer to him, leaning down over the table. "The front office here needs to be twelve feet high, but they need a two-foot suspended ceiling for the intercom and video equipment cables."

Robert's eyelids grew heavy with the scent of her perfume. She bent closer, her blouse brushing his hand. She continued talking, gesturing from sheet to sheet. Robert thought that if she didn't move away soon he would do something he'd be extremely sorry for. He concentrated on what she was saying, throwing his mind into the problem, away from his emotions.

Then Carol stood up. "What do you think?"

"I think," Robert said, locking eyes with her for a second, "that we have a problem. Might have to take a second look at the floor above. Either that, or convince them to settle for a ten-foot ceiling."

Carol fiddled with the top button on her blouse. "I was thinking, perhaps, that the cables could go in the wall. Better to lose a foot of floor space than height, don't you think?"

She's doing it on purpose, Robert suddenly thought. *She's throwing herself at me, for crying out loud. Or is she? Maybe it's just me. Too depressed over Lenore. I'm imagining things. Aren't I?*

Suddenly Carol laid a hand on his shoulder. "Look, Bob, I'll be honest with you. I heard your conversation with Lenore, and I'm not going to stand by and let you eat at some greasy-spoon burger joint. Come on, have dinner with me. We'll bring the plans and combine business with . . . with good food."

He almost said yes. He almost began thinking of a secluded little restaurant where no one would know them. He definitely was thinking about placing kisses on her smooth, white neck. But he just couldn't. Robert was as responsible to his marriage as he was to his career. He knew the difference between opportunity and indulgence.

"Sorry, Carol, maybe some other time," Robert said. "I guess I just need time alone. Besides, burgers are my favorite food."

"Just a thought," Carol said.

"Tell you what," Robert said. "I'll take the plans home and give you my thoughts in the morning. Right now I can say that your idea sounds like the best."

"Great," Carol said. She glanced at her watch. "Well, time to close up shop. See you in the a.m."

"See you, Carol."

And once again, he watched her walk slowly out of his office. He sat back with an explosive sigh.

Carol continued walking past her desk, past the reception area, down the hall and into the women's room. She went immediately to the sink and stood looking at herself in the large mirror.

Damn, she thought. *The man is made of ice, I swear. he is. What the heck is wrong with him? Other men would die for me, but somehow he's different, a tough nut.* Well, for one thing, he was married. But how did he manage to ignore her while he was still single? It didn't matter. He was married, and he seemed to be loyal. But there was a light at the end of the tunnel. That wimp he was married to was giving him a hard time. No one was more vulnerable than a frustrated husband, and no one is better at taking advantage of a situation like that than Carol.

I've got the equipment and I've got the brains. But if charm and sex appeal won't get through to him, what will? She knew it was working to some extent: she could see it in his face, in his eyes—his eyes were all over her! But she wasn't getting the man, the gorgeous, rich, creative, brilliant man. How could she snag him?

Start using more brains than body. And if that doesn't work, try something else. Because Robert Delaney will be mine if it's the last thing I do.

* * *

John Randolph was the first one to step inside the elevator. He studied the buttons for an extra couple of seconds before spotting the number he wanted. His finger missed on the first try, then he got it. He stepped back to the rear while sharply dressed business people crowded in around him.

The doors closed. John adjusted his tie, accidentally elbowing a lovely raven-haired woman to his left.

"Sorry," he said. "I really am sorry."

Her nose wrinkled, she frowned, then turned her face away, sharing a shake of the head with the man next to her.

John now concentrated on the lights above the door. *Don't want to miss my floor. Don't want to end up riding this thing all day. Up and down. Down and up.* He giggled and drew more disgusted stares.

It was five minutes before nine in the morning. When John had awakened that morning, he'd decided that today was the day to get his life together. Today he would clean up his life and get back on track. He was a lawyer, for crying out loud, and lawyers are supposed to be working, not groveling around without clients for—how long had it been?—six, eight months. He'd dressed and found himself out on the streets at seven o'clock. Nothing, of course, was open at seven o'clock. Too darn early, he'd thought. What now? There was only one place he could think of that was open at seven o'clock in the morning. Sammy's Pub. That was where John had spent the last two hours. Just John, the bartender and bourbon.

The Frame Enterprises elevator was nearly empty when it reached John's floor. He was proud that he'd recognized the number when it flashed yellow and the elevator stopped. He was okay.

"Scuse me," he said to the two patient men to his right. He stepped off the elevator not too elegantly.

Fear began to creep up on him. He adjusted his tie again. He noticed that his hands were shaking. *Got to do it,* he thought. *Get going before you change your blasted mind.*

He moved forward with strides a good foot longer than he would normally take. A blond receptionist greeted him with a grin.

"Good morning," she said. "May I help you?"

"I'd . . . I'd like to see Steve Frame," he said.

The odor of liquor wafted over her and her smile faded. "Do you have an appointment?"

"No, no appointment. But he knows me. My name's John Randolph."

The blonde didn't try to hide the astonishment on her face. "Oh, Mr. Randolph. I didn't recognize you, I'm sorry. Let me see if Mr. Frame is in." She buzzed Steve's office. "Mr. Frame? Mr. Randolph is here to see you. . . . I see, yes, I'll tell him." She turned to John. "I'm sorry, Mr. Frame says he's in conference. He can't see you today."

John looked her square in the eye. "Bull," he said. Then he turned and walked past the desk, through the glass doors, down the hall and straight into Steve Frame's office. Steve was sitting at his large oak desk, alone.

"Who the hell let you in!" Steve demanded, rising.

"Sorry. I have to talk to you, I really do, Steve."

"You're drunk," Steve spat. "Nine in the morning and you're drunk. Get out, John. Now."

"Please, Steve, just listen, okay? Just listen, please."

Steve saw that John was on the verge of tears. The

man he'd known for many years, the lawyer who'd betrayed him, was falling apart before his very eyes.

"Sit down," Steve said. "Make it fast."

"Thanks, Steve," John said, sitting down.

"Well?"

John ran his fingers through his hair. "Pat threw me out of the house, Steve. I'm living in a motel."

Part of Steve's heart went out to John, but he didn't give in. "I can't help you with that, John."

John went on. "It's my drinking, I guess. Got nothing to do anymore. One minute I was the best lawyer in town, now I'm a nothing, a bum. I'm losing everything. Now my wife throws me out of my own house, out of her life."

Steve was getting angry. "I can't say that you don't deserve it, John. I spent nearly six months in prison because of you. I thought you were my friend, and you were on my payroll for many years. But you turned on me, John."

"I had to," John said. "I'm a lawyer and supposed to be honest. You broke the law and I had to do something. I had to!"

"John, you're drunk. This is doing neither of us any good. Go on, get out, get sober, then call me."

John stood and strode up to Steve's desk. "You think life has been a picnic for me while you were in jail? Huh? You think I can get work after you fired me, disgraced me, told everybody and their brother that I double-crossed you? I'm ruined. Sure, you can sit there with your empire, nice and cozy, but look at me, Steve. I . . . I need your help, Steve."

John began to cry softly.

"John . . ."

"You have to take me back, Steve. It's the only

way. Look at me! I'm a drunk. Help me get back on my feet. Give me a chance again. I'm sorry they locked you up because of me—but I was your lawyer! You hired me to be honest, and even though it got you busted, I had to do my job. But it's all over now, isn't it? Things can be the same again. Gimme another chance, okay?"

"John, I can't. Things aren't the same. You're not my friend anymore, John. I don't even know how good a lawyer you are anymore. I feel sorry for you, for Pat, but it's up to you to knock off this drinking and pull your life together. Sorry, I can't do it."

John was crying openly now. "Please! I'm begging, Steve. I'm on my knees. Don't hold it against me because I stuck to ethics and turned you in. God, that's old news now, Steve."

Steve blew up. "Where were your ethics when Rachel was blackmailing me? When she married me under false pretenses? Even the court agreed with me, John. But I didn't think they would, so I bribed someone to get true justice. But I didn't really have to, did I? No, but I didn't know that then. Nothing would have come out of it, no one would have been hurt, the results of the trial would have been exactly the same. But one of my best friends, a lawyer hired to defend me, turned on me and I lost four months of my life in a cell. I can't forgive you, John, and I will never hire you back. Get ahold of yourself. You say you're a good lawyer—then prove it. Get out there and work. You don't need me."

"I do!" John said. "I belong here at Frame. You've gotta take me back, Steve! I've got no place else to go!"

Steve lifted the phone and spoke quickly. "Security? Steve Frame. Come up here immediately."

John stumbled over to Steve. Steve tried to push him off.

"Give me a break, Steve. You can forgive me, you know you can. Please, please."

Steve knew that somewhere inside him there might be forgiveness. But the whole thing was too recent and John was in such a pitiful condition that all he felt was disgusted and angered.

"No," Steve said flatly.

"So," John said, straightening up. "You're out for your ounce of flesh. You're out for revenge, is that it?"

"Of course not."

Two brawny security men in uniforms came into Steve's office. Steve nodded toward John, and they moved swiftly, taking John's arms and hustling him toward the door.

"It's not enough you fired me and ruined me!" John was yelling. "Now you're out for my blood! You're a coward! At least I stood up for what I believed in! You *deserved* to go to jail and you know it! Revenge is a coward's game, Steve! And you—"

The door closed, leaving Steve Frame in silence, John's words still ringing harshly and bitterly in his ears.

Chapter Nine
New Beginnings

It was the last day of August. A light but pleasant rain had fallen in the morning, but now the sun had broken through to warm the damp earth and fill the air with early breezes of autumn.

After lunch, Mac and Rachel sat in the den of Mac's mansion giggling and hugging over the two hundred photos they'd taken during their glorious honeymoon.

"You look very French in a beret," Rachel said. "Dashing, sexy."

"You think so?" Mac said. "Maybe I should grow one of those thin mustaches."

"You do and I'll kill you," Rachel said.

Mac laughed, and they flipped to the next photo.

Rachel loved Mac's home. It suited her perfectly, the hired help loved her and Mac helped her make it her own by insisting on hanging her favorite paintings and rearranging things to suit her tastes.

But most of all, Rachel loved knowing she had a

home with a man who loved her, who would always be there. It'd been so long, so long that she'd been alone and desperate and confused. Now her life, at long last, was in order. The future couldn't look brighter.

A cocker spaniel puppy suddenly burst into the room.

"Lucky!" Mac said to the cute little dog. "What are you doing in here? Come to mess up the rug again?"

"Oh, Mac!" Rachel said.

Soon Jamie came rushing in, dangling an old sock in his fingers, which Lucky immediately started nipping and tugging.

"You should have seen, Mom," Jamie said to Rachel. "Lucky couldn't stand up on the kitchen tiles! It was a riot! He kept slipping and sliding like crazy!"

Rachel could only sit back and let her son's happiness soak in. Now, after all this time, Rachel and Jamie were finally together again in a house, in a home, with a family.

What have I been missing? Rachel wondered. She had asked herself this question hundreds of times over the past few weeks. And her answer, as always, was: everything.

The puppy was Mac's present to Jamie when he'd shyly come, suitcases in hand, to move in with his mom and her new husband. It didn't take long for Jamie to adjust. The boy must have been longing for a home with his mother for a long time. Jamie's joy brought an extra depth of satisfaction and love to Mac's and Rachel's marriage.

The only thorn in the side of their happiness was

Iris. Iris had been dredging up all the dirt she could about Rachel and spreading it all over town. And when Iris ran out of dirt, she invented her own. Yes, Rachel knew that, although she had gained a happy family, she had also made an enemy.

"Get that pooch outside before he does something you'll have to clean up," Mac said to Jamie.

"Let's go, Lucky!" Jamie said, dangling the tempting sock behind him as he ran out of the room, Lucky on his heels.

The phone rang.

Mac reached to his right and lifted the receiver. "Hello? . . . What? . . . Holy mackerel! . . . A what? . . . Holy mackerel! . . . We'll be right over!" Mac hung up.

"What is it?" Rachel said.

"It's your mother," Mac said. "She had her baby!"

"Really! Is she okay and everything?"

"Gil said it couldn't have gone smoother," Mac said.

"Boy or girl?"

"Girl."

"A girl," Rachel reflected. "My sister. I have a sister—and I'm old enough to be her mother. Gosh, her grandmother!"

"What's that make me? Father Time? Quit feeling your age, and let's get going! The kid isn't getting any younger, you know!"

Gil, in his Bay City policeman's uniform, was standing in the hall outside the hospital room when Mac and Rachel arrived. Gil was beaming.

"It's great, isn't it? I can hardly believe I'm a daddy. I feel twenty-five again."

"Congratulations," Mac said. He shook Gil's hand

heartily and Rachel gave him a warm kiss and hug. "So what are you doing standing out here in the hall?"

"Ada just came back from recovery. She's awake and strong and happy. Nancy's in there with her."

"Who's Nancy?" Rachel asked.

"My new daughter, that's who," Gil said.

"So, I repeat," Mac said, "what are you doing out here?"

Gil scratched his head. "I'm not really sure. I think they wanted me to wait out here until Ada was settled in. Hey, Mac, am I supposed to give out cigars for a girl? Or is it only for a boy?"

"Darned if I know," Mac said.

Just then a nurse popped her head out the door, smiled and said, "Come in, Daddy."

Everyone entered. Ada was propped up, still a little groggy but fighting it off and staring at the small, sleeping bundle in her arms. She looked up radiantly.

"Come here, everyone. Look at my beautiful daughter."

"What a stunner!" Mac said.

"Oh, Mom, I'm so happy for you," Rachel said, kissing Ada.

"Thank you, honey," Ada said, squeezing her older daughter's hand.

Mac hugged Rachel, purposefully smiling at her.

"I think she looks like you, Ada," Gil said.

"She's got your chin, though," Ada said.

"And Rachel's eyes," Gil said.

After a few more minutes, the nurse said, "I think it's time for mother and baby to get a little rest and nourishment. You can all come back later this afternoon. Visiting hours here are until ten o'clock."

Everyone said their good-byes and headed out of

the room, arm in arm. Not wanting to break their happy mood and good feelings, they decided to go down to the coffee shop.

Gil leaned over his steaming cup of coffee and spoke to Rachel. "You know, your mom is really proud of you, Rachel. And, indirectly, of Mac, too."

"Thanks, I think," Mac said, laughing.

"What do you mean?" Rachel asked.

"Well," Gil began, searching for words, "ever since this old coot here came into your life, it seems to your mom that, well, that you've changed, I guess. Anyway, she feels a lot closer to you lately, Rachel. It's clear to everybody that you're happy, and you're wearing it well. Your mother really loves you, Rachel, and she kind of feels like she finally has you back again. Does that make any sense?"

"It makes all the sense in the world, Gil," Rachel said. "Thanks for telling me. I feel like we've all somehow got a new start—me, you and Ada, Mac here and especially Jamie. I am happy, probably for the first time in my life."

And Gil and Ada weren't the only ones to notice it. Even Rachel's staunchest past adversaries were being convinced that there was a new Rachel in town. People who once couldn't say anything but vindictive and catty things about her were now finding themselves inviting her to parties and commenting on what a nice couple she and Mac made. Scandalous Rachel was now doing things like joining the P.T.A. and getting involved with Jamie's education. She was shopping in town, pausing to chat with shop owners and bankers. Yes, the talk of the town was certainly in Rachel's favor.

But people, especially in a small, affluent town like

Bay City, thoroughly enjoy the darker side of their society. And the town's good graces would possibly not have been so quickly lavished on Rachel if people did not have a new, juicy scandal to whet their appetites: Iris Carrington.

Everyone knew of Iris's feud with her father and her loathing of his and Rachel's relationship. Everyone knew of her vows to explode the marriage and wreak vengeance on Rachel. So, quite suddenly, Rachel now had the town's sympathy and Iris was the town's new prey.

All of this, including the birth of Rachel's baby sister, had its effect on Mac's and Rachel's relationship. Every once in a while, Mac gave in to his deep regret over Iris, and Rachel would be there to help him through it. But most of the time, Mac accepted the whole thing at face value. He was old enough to understand that people must be responsible for their own lives and their own choices. Iris's problems were not his to solve, they were Iris's. He had his own life to live, and if loving Iris was not enough for her, then she would have to deal with her problem on her own.

But Rachel was still young enough to be confused by the effect others' lives had on hers.

When Gil excused himself to check in at the police station, Mac and Rachel remained in the coffee shop. As usual, Mac was on Rachel's wavelength.

"Be happy for your mom," Mac said. "Think of Nancy as your mother's daughter, not your sister."

"But she is my sister, Mac. It's depressing to me; I'm sorry, but it is. I feel as if time has gone by and I haven't even noticed."

"Look at it this way: you're getting a second chance," Mac said. "You're going to be very valuable to little Nancy as she grows, Rachel. If anyone can help her through the tough times, you can. She's lucky to have a sister like you."

"But who's going to help me?" Rachel said.

"Ahh," Mac said, knowingly.

"What's that mean?"

"First, Rachel, you don't need help anymore. And if you do, I'm here. And your mother's there, too. You kind of feel like you're losing your mother, don't you? Don't answer, I know you do. She's the only one you've had to turn to for quite a few years. Well, she's still there for you. Be happy for her. What has she had in her life lately? She's been a housewife married to a cop. Sure, they've been happy, but think about how they felt when you took Jamie away to live with us. I'll bet you a nickel they would have been pretty depressed about that if Ada wasn't expecting. And now that everything's fine and Nancy's in the world, I'd say that just about all the best things that could have happened to all of us have happened. All of us share a lot, have shared a lot, so what's your problem?"

Rachel gave Mac a tight squeeze and a kiss. "I love you, I love you, I love you, Mac Cory."

"Couldn't live without me."

"Never."

"Think I'm the kindest and most handsome guy in the world?"

"You are."

"I'd be even handsomer with one of those little thin mustaches."

When Mac and Rachel arrived back home, Simon, the head butler, was waiting.

"Sir, something's happened," Simon said.

"Calm down, Simon," Mac said. "What's up?"

"Your daughter was here."

"Iris?"

"Yes, sir. She and three men I can only describe as filthy."

"Filthy?"

"Moving men. She came to retrieve her things. She left this note."

Simon handed Mac an envelope. Mac tore it open and read:

Mac—

Since I have had my own apartment for quite some time now, I've finally arranged to get the rest of my belongings out of your house and your life.

I have also laid claim to a few other things that I feel fully entitled to, things that I have lived with for many years—things that I cannot bear having violated by the woman you call your wife.

If you object to anything I've taken, don't call me. Call your lawyer, for I fully intend taking you to court over the slightest objection.

My keys to your house are enclosed. I think it's a shame that you've divorced yourself from your only daughter because of a childish whim. You have hurt me deeply and you have angered me.

But I hold you only partly to blame. You don't know what you're doing, and you will pay for it in the end because of your Mrs.—a woman who has ruined more lives than you'll ever know, including mine.

Iris

"Mac," Rachel said, taking his arm, "I'm sorry." But Mac was in one of his strong moods. "She'll get over it. Iris's trouble is that she never grew up, never accepted her life as it is, always wanted more than she had. Come on, let's see what she hauled off."

Suddenly Rachel had a thought. "Jamie! He must have been here when Iris stormed in."

"Don't worry," Simon said. "I took Jamie to my quarters and he played with the dog. I doubt if he even knew she was here."

Rachel sighed. "Simon, you're a lifesaver."

Mac had wandered off into the living room. "Well, she snatched my Renoir."

"The nerve!" Rachel said. "That must be worth thousands."

Mac chuckled. "Hundreds of thousands."

As they moved around the house, Mac pointed out various valuables that Iris had taken—silver, antiques, a few more paintings and lithographs—but the biggest shock awaited them upstairs.

Rachel's entire wardrobe was strewn all over the floor. Her jewelry, undergarments and everything she'd had in the drawers of her bureau were scattered around the room.

"My God!" Rachel said.

"She wanted the bureau," Mac pointed out. "It was her grandmother's and a favorite of hers. I guess Iris couldn't resist causing a bit of a mess while she was at it."

"It looks like we were robbed," Rachel said. "This is horrible."

Mac stepped forward and took Rachel in his arms. "I'll tell you something. It's more horrible for Iris than it is for us. She thinks she got some sort of revenge here. But the one thing she can't steal or mess up is us. Big deal, she's taken a few odds and ends. Let her have them. I wouldn't care if she'd cleaned the place out. I've got you, you've got me, we've got a great life. All Iris has is *things*. That's the path she's chosen, and if that's what makes her happy, so be it."

"Mac, you are so right," Rachel said.

They kissed, then began to make a list of gifts for the baby and Ada.

Chapter Ten
Passion and Pity

Lenore felt something coming on. A cold, the flu, allergies, a bug, depression—she didn't know.

After she'd risen and shuffled into the bathroom at 7:00 A.M., the mirror told her that today work was out of the question. She looked very old today, she thought. Very tired. Her long sandy hair, usually lustrous, was dull. Her crisp blue eyes were rimmed with red. Her lips puffy. She could afford a day off. Besides, she felt she needed it.

Robert, on the other hand, was gung ho this morning.

"Bob, I'm staying home today," Lenore said.

"Not feeling well?"

"Not too."

"Sorry to hear it. Wish I had that luxury. Big things happening today. The Wilshire and Company closing is today. I hope those guys don't have any surprises for me." He hurried into the bathroom and, just before closing the door, he leaned back out and said, "Two eggs, no bacon and toast would be terrific." He closed the door and turned on the shower.

Lenore sat on the edge of the bed, unable to tear her stare off the bathroom door. Just once she wished he'd think. Why couldn't he make his own breakfast? Perhaps he didn't hear her. Maybe his mind was whirling with the day ahead. Lenore gave him the benefit of the doubt and walked out to prepare his breakfast and Wally's.

The heat of the stove made her dizzy enough so that she had to sit down. Something *was* wrong, but somehow Lenore knew it wasn't a bug or the flu.

"Oh, no!" She leaped up and turned off the gas beneath the frying pan. Bob couldn't stand, and wouldn't eat, overdone fried eggs. These were a shade too well-done. Should she throw them out before he yelled and screamed? Maybe he wouldn't notice.

She slid the eggs onto a plate and covered them with another plate. Her heart was racing and she felt a hot blush covering her cheeks. *Fear,* she thought. *I'm afraid, deathly afraid, that Bob won't like his eggs. He's got me trained.*

A minute later, Robert came out in a dark-blue suit, adjusting his tie.

"Really sorry, no time for breakfast. You eat them, you look like you could use them."

"I don't like eggs, Bob, you know that."

"Shouldn't you be getting ready?"

"I told you, I'm staying home today. Taking the day off. I don't feel all that well."

"Oh, right," Robert said. "Maybe you do need a rest. Watch some soaps. Laze around. If you think of it, could you squeeze in a little sock-mending?"

The heat hadn't left Lenore's face, and now it entered her voice. "Bob, why don't you just pick up some new ones?"

"A penny saved, and all that."

"I'm not a housewife, Bob, and I'm not going to sit around here all day, feeling lousy, darning your socks. You've already dragged me out of bed to make a breakfast you're not eating."

Bob walked up to her and took her face in his hands. "Sorry, honey, I've got no time to argue with a grouchy wife."

"I'm not grouchy. I'm fed up. Why don't you make your own breakfast for a change, and darn your own socks? I didn't marry you to be your slave, Bob. I don't want my life to revolve around yours, I want to have my own life, too."

"Wow," Robert said viciously. "Sorry if I'm expecting too much. But it's too early to discuss such important matters."

"You still think I'm going to quit Frame, don't you?"

"Look, Lenore, I've got to be going."

"Don't you? Well, I'm not, Bob."

He ignored her, snatched up his briefcase and headed for the door. "By the way, what kind of delicious dinner do you have planned?"

Lenore blew up. "What's wrong with you? I'm sick today, or haven't you been listening? Doesn't it even dawn on you that maybe I shouldn't have to slave for your dinner tonight? Don't you see what you're doing?"

Robert glared at her. "Yes, I do see what I'm doing. I'm leaving for work. Have a nice day doing nothing." He turned, opened the door, stepped through, then slammed it behind him.

Lenore collapsed in tears. She felt angry, humiliated, belittled. But most of all she raged at herself because she truly did feel guilty over not wanting to make his dinner or darn his socks. Weren't those things that a wife should do? *No!* her other self screamed. *You're a career woman, not a maid.* But, she countered, *if it makes him happy? If spit-shining his shoes every morning made him happy, would you do it?* There's a limit, Lenore. Get a hold of yourself. Find yourself again. Don't let him turn you into a cog in the wheel of his life. *But what's wrong? Why do I feel this way?* Maybe you don't know your husband as well as you think you do.

Or, she thought, *maybe there's something wrong with me.*

On his way to work, Robert fumed. He was completely blind to his domineering side. He had no idea what he was inflicting upon his vulnerable wife. He had rigid ideas about what a wife should be, ideas so rigid that he didn't even bother to question them. He considered them facts of life. But the fact of life that eluded him was that he was crushing an intelligent, ambitious and caring woman who truly loved him.

So, he fumed. He didn't realize he hadn't yet made space in his life for Lenore. His opinions were always the ones that counted. His tastes and preferences were all that mattered. His ways of decorating the house, fixing meals, making love were the best and only ways. He resisted accepting Lenore's opinions or preferences. He had no curiosity about what Lenore thought, how she viewed the world, what she considered beautiful, ugly or sexy.

Therefore, Robert was frustrated and he had no idea why—except that he knew his wife was the cause of his pain.

Robert carried his angst throughout the day, being overly stubborn in his negotiations, snapping at his co-workers and, overall, dreading going home.

So when Lenore phoned him at four forty-five, he

was in no mood to be pleasant. Lenore, on the other hand, had been accumulating guilt all day. She wanted to make peace.

"Hi, Bob, it's me," Lenore said. "I had a good rest today, and I thought I'd call to see what you want for dinner."

"I don't want another fight," he said.

"We'll have a nice evening, I promise."

"I don't know what I want," Robert said. "I'm nowhere near hungry—work has piled up. I can't think."

"We have a nice ham, how about that?"

Robert sighed. "You know I don't like ham very much."

"I forgot. Sorry. So, what do you want?"

"You decide."

"Well, if you had left it up to me, I would have chosen ham. Boy, would that have been a mistake. You're so hard to please."

Robert sighed again. "Lenore, don't you know me by now? Can't you make a little decision like dinner without me?"

Lenore caught herself gritting her teeth. "You're the fussy one, not me. I'm giving you a choice, *your* choice, so you have no right to complain."

Robert was so angry he couldn't get his thoughts together. "It looks like I'll be working late anyway, so you and Wally go ahead without me. That ought to avoid another confrontation."

"Will you eat? What time will you be home?"

"I'll be home, Lenore, whenever I get home. When the work is done. When the job is finished. What, am I suddenly on a timetable or something?"

"Consideration, that's all I'm asking, Bob. It's no

worse than your asking for fried eggs cooked exactly three and a half minutes."

"That makes no sense, Lenore, and this conversation is getting ridiculous. Don't wait up for me." Robert slammed down the phone, greatly relieved to be rid of Lenore's voice.

What the heck is going wrong with her? he wondered. *She doesn't understand me at all.*

Robert looked up and, again, the shapely figure of Carol Lamonte was in the doorway.

"Come on in, Carol," Robert said. "Tell me what a great guy I am. I can use it."

"You're a great guy, Bob," Carol said, then thought: *if he only knew how much I mean it.*

"Thanks, I feel better already. What can I do for you?"

"We had a meeting, remember?" she said. "Quarter of five?"

"Oh, geez, right," Robert said. "It's not that I forgot, I just got distracted."

"There's more bad news," Carol said. "The blueprints we were supposed to be discussing? I left them at home this morning."

Robert was getting back into his professional working mood. "At home, huh? We really have to settle those tonight, Carol. The clients will be in in the morning."

"I know. I'm really sorry," Carol said. "But wait a sec. I've got a great idea. You want a treat? I made some lasagna last night—it's always best the next day. Come on over to my townhouse—we'll eat and look at the blues. How about it?"

Robert considered. "It's either that or I wait here while you go home to get them, which is ridiculous.

Okay, you're on. And let's go now, I'm starved. Thanks, Carol."

"Forget it. I'll get my things."

Carol walked back to her desk, turned to make sure Robert could not see her, then bent and tucked the blueprints deeper into her oversized bag.

Carol's townhouse was spectacular, and Robert said so. Spacious first floor, tastefully decorated with cozy furniture with a pink-and-tan theme. To the left was a spiral staircase leading up to a balcony and the bedroom beyond. She had used both glass and mirrors to great advantage. Robert felt immediately comfortable and relaxed.

"Drink?" Carol asked.

"Wine would be terrific."

"Coming right up. I'll stick the lasagna in the microwave while I'm at it."

Carol hummed in the kitchen. *What a stroke of luck,* she thought. *Get him while he's down. What's a great guy like Robert doing with a witch like Lenore in the first place? Obviously, she doesn't understand him. And Bob does need to be understood—creative people, successful people, need special care. Now what Bob needs is reassurance, someone he can be with who wants to love him on his own terms. Someone to ease away the pains of a painful marriage. Me.*

She'd sneaked the blueprints out of her bag, and now she brought them to the coffee table before Robert. They settled down on her sectional sofa, wine in hand, and scanned the blues.

An hour later, with business settled, they moved to the dining room to consume the delicious lasagna and another two glasses of wine. Robert finally loosened up and chatted with much animation, reducing Carol to laughter many times. Both of them were touchers in conversation, laying a hand on an arm, a wrist, a shoulder as they made a point or reacted to something. They got along famously. All of this filled Carol with confidence.

Robert couldn't remember enjoying himself more in quite some time. The atmosphere of the place, the great food and the lovely, free-spirited woman combined to sweep away his worries.

They moved back to the sofa for coffee. Carol put on an album of Gershwin. They kicked off their shoes.

Robert noticed how differently Carol looked and acted away from the office. Here, she was softer, more open with her smile. Her mind was a quick one and easily kept up with him as he continued his banter. And with her long, shapely legs stretched out to the coffee table, attractive toes wiggling, she was a sight almost too inviting to resist.

Carol made a comment about the music, laying her hand on his. She left it there.

Robert moved his eyes to hers, his smile fading. He did not move his hand. Carol smiled warmly into his eyes, then slid her fingers under his hand and took his palm in hers.

She rose, gave a little tug, and Robert rose with her. Slowly, she walked toward the spiral staircase. Robert was mesmerized, heated, unable to make a decision.

Suddenly she stopped and turned. She leaned toward him, holding her eyes on his, and kissed him lightly on the cheek. She released his hand and proceeded up the staircase. Robert watched her go, his heart racing, his mind working.

She paused at the top and looked back down at him. Then she turned and walked toward the bedroom, unbuttoning the back button of her skirt.

Slowly, Robert climbed the staircase.

Hours later, after Robert had gone, Carol knew this was merely the beginning. If she had her way, Robert would be back, night after night. Then he'd be hers. But before she could totally claim him, before Robert would feel free to love her, there was one small problem she had not yet solved: Lenore.

What to do about Lenore? Actually, she mused, there was only one thing to do. And after that, Robert would come running straight to her.

The first day of autumn arrived on a blustery, chilly wind. No hairdo in town was safe on a day like this, so most of the usually bustling shopping district streets were fairly empty. It was the kind of day that most of Bay City enjoyed indoors, visiting friends or throwing parties.

Steve and Alice Frame were doing neither. They were in the back seat of a gleaming black Lincoln limousine, heading for the hospital to visit Dr. Russ Matthews and check on little Dennis's progress.

Russ greeted them in his office with a wide grin.

"Alice, terrific to see you. How are you, Steve? Come in, please."

Russ gestured to two chairs, and Steve and Alice took seats.

"Russ," Alice said, "you look like you've lost weight."

"A few pounds. I took up handball and it seems to be working."

"We'll have to play a game," Steve said.

"Only if you promise to take it easy on me. I'm a beginner."

Steve chuckled.

"How's Dennis?" Alice asked.

"Recovering splendidly," Russ said. "He's a strong boy, both in body and will. He's been asking for you, but you'll have to put it off for today. He's in physical therapy right now."

"Oh, too bad. I wanted to see him."

"Eliot's been asking about you, too," Russ said.

"How is he?" asked Steve. "Gosh, I haven't seen him in ages."

"Terrific. Always working on a new book," Russ said.

Just then a knock boomed, and Iris Carrington entered.

"A party!" she said.

Alice rose stiffly, defensively. If there was one person she did not want to see, it was Iris. She was certain that Iris still blamed her for breaking up Iris's and Eliot's marriage. Alice didn't trust Iris an inch.

"How are you, Alice?" Iris said.

"Fine. You?"

"I think I'm fine," Iris said. "Am I fine, Russ?"

"Healthy as an ox," Russ said, trying to soothe the tension in the room with a bit of levity.

"Not an animal I usually identify with," Iris said, smiling. "Well, I won't invade your conversation any more. Can I see Dennis, Russ?"

"Sorry, not now, Iris. He's in physical therapy."

"Again? You trying to turn him into Mr. Universe or something?"

That caught Steve by surprise and he laughed loudly.

"Why, thank you, Mr. Frame," Iris said.

Alice thought, *she sure is in rare form today.*

"You know, Steve," Iris said, "I was just thinking about you today."

"Really?"

"Sort of. Actually I was thinking about your ex-wife. Rachel. Have you seen her lately?"

"No."

"You'd be quite surprised," Iris said. "She married my father, you know. My very old father."

"I know," Steve said.

"And has she changed!" Iris said. "It's all over town what a nice, sweet woman Rachel has become. They say it's a miracle. Tell me, Steve—and you, too, Russ, since you were married to Rachel many moons ago —would either of you describe Rachel as a nice, sweet woman?"

"Iris, that's enough," Alice said. "Steve, I think it's about time we got going."

"I'm sorry, I'm sorry," Iris said. "Really, I'm sorry. Why take it out on you folks? It's upsetting when your own father, once a very nice man, hooks up with someone the world knows to be a . . . well, not quite an upstanding woman."

Russ took a step toward Iris. "Iris, you know, it is possible for people to change. Even Rachel. It seems like your dad is a good influence. Why not give Rachel a chance?"

Surprisingly, Iris softened. "I guess it's not in my nature to do so. Not after all that's happened in the town over the years. I guess I feel like Rachel has stolen something from me. It's her pattern, isn't it? Stealing affections?"

"Iris," Alice said, "no matter what you think about me, I do understand what you're saying. I do care."

Iris was suspicious. "You want to be my friend, Alice?"

Russ snapped, "That wasn't fair, Iris."

"Never mind," Alice said. "I asked for it. We really do have to be going."

Steve reached over and shook Russ's hand. "Good to see you, Russ. I'll call you, set up an appointment for a court. Any time best for you?"

"Friday looks clear. Morning."

"You got it."

Iris walked over and stood directly in front of Alice. "Russ is right, it wasn't fair." She held out her hand. Alice took it. They shook briefly.

"Good-bye, Iris," Alice said. "I hope things work out."

"As long as my father is married to that woman, I kind of doubt it."

Steve and Alice left. Walking down the corridor, Steve turned to Alice.

"I'd say Iris has a few emotional problems, wouldn't you?"

Alice nodded. "And one of them is that she's in love with Russ."

Steve stopped in his tracks. "What? How could you possibly know that?"

"First of all, if Russ hadn't been there, Iris would have spit in my face. She hates me and probably always will. Second, I know Iris possibly better than any other woman does. I've worked closely with her ex-husband, Eliot, and I've known Iris for years. I also know Russ—he helped me a great deal while you were in prison. Believe me, she's got it bad for Russ."

"But Iris and Russ?" Steve said, scratching his head. "Impossible!"

"That's exactly what the whole town said about Mac and Rachel."

Mac said, "Let's go slumming."

"Huh?" Rachel said.

Minutes before, Mac had discovered Rachel toying with the dark-chestnut strands of her shimmering hair at the large foyer mirror. He'd come up and kissed her on the back of the neck.

"What are you up to?" Mac had asked.

"Deciding how short I want to have my hair cut," she'd replied.

"Oh, no!" Mac had grumbled. "Jamie's enough —we don't need two boys around here."

Now Mac led her outside onto their back porch, overlooking a small pond and the tennis courts off to the left.

"I feel like going out," Mac said, "but not to some fancy place. Let's go someplace else; someplace where we can let our hair down—before both of us lose it."

Rachel giggled and hugged his arm. "Okay, where?"

"How about Taco Bill's?"

"That Tex-Mex place?"

"Sound good?" Mac said. "They've always got some kind of good country-western band there, good food, good beer. Are we on?"

"We're on."

They went back inside and Mac called for Simon on the intercom. Soon, Simon arrived.

"Simon, keep an eye on Jamie and the mutt for us, will you? We'll be eating out tonight."

"I'll be happy to," Simon said. "Jamie and I are teaching Lucky some wonderful tricks."

"You are?" Rachel said. "What have you taught him so far?"

"He's on the verge of learning to sit," Simon said.

"I think he knows that one, Simon," Mac said. "The filthy dog's been sitting all over the house."

Taco Bill's had a huge sign out front: THE LAST DAY OF SEPTEMBER LONE STAR SPECIAL STEAK—ALL YOU CAN EAT AND DRINK —ONLY $15.95!

"My kind of place," Mac said.

Rachel shook her head and they entered Taco Bill's. People in Bay City got a big kick out of Taco Bill's, dressing up to suit the atmosphere. The huge, wooden dining area was dotted with customers' ten-gallon hats and leather vests. The tables were of dark, well-used pine, the chairs were old-style rail-backs. On the walls were Old West frying pans, other cooking utensils and reproductions of Wanted posters and billboards. Beside each wooden support beam were huge barrels of peanuts. The long, oak bar spanned the length of the back wall, on which hung a huge oil painting of a reclining nude.

The bar was already crowded. The band, "The Bad Boys," was set up on a small platform stage to the right, playing their hearts out on a country song Rachel knew but couldn't remember the words to. On the deeply scuffed dance floor, couples twirled and yipped and spun.

A woman in a leather vest, a plaid skirt and a pink cowboy hat approached them. "Table for two?"

"Thank ya, ya pretty little filly," Mac said.

Rachel giggled and gave him an elbow in the side.

A few minutes later, they placed their order —nachos, burritos, enchiladas, refried beans, the works.

"This was a great idea," Rachel said. "What fun!"

"Wanna dance?" Mac said.

Rachel shook her head. "I want to just watch for a while. And will you please drop that horrible cowboy accent?"

"Glad to oblige, ma'am," Mac said.

Two tall glasses of beer arrived. Mac and Rachel toasted each other and took a drink.

"Well, I'll be!" Mac suddenly said.

"What?" Rachel said.

"Is it? Why, it is! I see an old friend of mine. Haven't seen him in years."

"Who?"

"There, over there at the end of the bar," Mac said, pointing. "John Randolph. You know, the lawyer who works with Steve Frame."

Rachel's jaw dropped. She suddenly realized that she had never told Mac the full story of her divorce trial from Steve Frame or of John's fate. John had defended Steve against her, and Rachel was certain that she was the last person on earth whom John wished to see, especially now.

"Mac, listen, I have to tell you something," Rachel said.

But Mac wasn't listening. He was already on his feet, heading over toward John. All Rachel could do was sit and watch.

Mac slapped John heartily on the back. John reacted slowly, simply turning toward Mac, recognizing him, giving him a feeble smile. They shook hands. Mac gestured toward their table. *No*, Rachel thought, *please don't ask him over*. Too late. John was being dragged, drink in hand, right toward her.

"Look what the cat dragged in," Mac said to Rachel, presenting John.

And John looked horrible. Sunken eyes, skinny, defeated.

"Hello, John," Rachel said.

"Hi, Rachel," John said. Then John surprisingly placed a hand on Rachel's shoulder. "I never got the chance to say how happy I am for you and Mac."

Rachel was shocked. It was because of her trial with Steve that John had lost everything, and here he was making peace.

"Thank you, John. That means a lot to me. Sit down, please."

As John skidded out a chair and sat down, Mac and Rachel exchanged knowing glances. They both knew John was drunk.

"Have you eaten?" Mac asked John.

"I was going to. I guess I forgot."

"Well, this is your lucky day," Mac said. "We've ordered enough for an army, and you are more than welcome to dig in."

"Thanks, Mac," John said. "You look great."

And the ever-frank Mac replied, "Well, you don't. In fact, you look terrible."

John moved his gaze to Rachel. "Doesn't he know?"

"No," Rachel said.

"What don't I know?" Mac said.

Rachel explained. She told Mac about her divorce from Steve Frame, even confessing that she had tricked him into marrying him. She explained how John had defended Steve, then later discovered that Steve had bribed a witness, and then how John had turned Steve in and how Steve was subsequently sent to prison.

John took over from there. "And it was then that my whole life fell into a heap. Steve fired me, naturally, and when Steve Frame fires you, you don't work anywhere else, believe me. I won't try to fool you—I started drinking. Still am. Seriously drinking, too. So seriously that Pat threw me out of the house two months ago."

They were interrupted by the arrival of the food. It was a Tex-Mex feast. As they ate, Mac asked John questions about how he'd tried to find work, how Pat was and what his plans were. John merely shrugged at each query and didn't say much at all. But the food was energizing him, taking the edge off his drunken state and animating him.

"I'm a lawyer, right?" John said. "I'm supposed to be honest, right? So what did I do wrong? I stuck to the law, Steve broke it and I helped enforce it."

"I'm to blame," Rachel said. "If it wasn't for me, you would never have been in that trial."

"That is correct," John said. "But you are not to blame, Rachel. Regardless of your motives, you got your punishment in court. It was Steve who broke the letter of the law. That's what laws are for!"

"I agree," Mac said, chewing. "Frame's got no right ruining your life because you had guts enough to be an honest man."

John looked up at Mac with wide eyes. "You know, Mac, you are the first person—and I mean the very first person—to agree with me, to see my side."

"This stupid town protects its own," Mac said. "Steve Frame, king of the hill, could have killed fifty people, and if you put him behind bars, you'd be the villain."

As Mac and John talked on, Rachel's heart went out to John Randolph. The poor man was once a brilliant lawyer, and now he had nothing but a bottle.

No friends, no family, no work, no life. He was defeated emotionally and physically.

It was time, Rachel thought, to patch up a piece of her past. To make right at least one of her wrongs.

"John," Rachel said, "I want you to put down that glass. No more booze, starting right now."

John gnashed his teeth. "You, too? I've been getting lectures from everyone, from the priest on the street to bartenders all over town."

"John," she said, "I'm not going to lecture you. I'm going to help you."

Mac slapped the table. "Great idea. I'm surprised that I didn't think of it, too."

"Where are you staying, John?" Rachel asked.

"Lately I've been at the rooming house over on Ashwood."

"Well, Mr. Randolph, pack your bags. You're coming to stay with us."

John shook his head. "No, no I couldn't. I . . . I don't even know if I can stop drinking. No, I'd better not. I'm a hopeless case."

"Every case has a defense," Mac said. "And if it doesn't have a defense, it has a loophole. I don't know what I'm getting at, but Rachel's right. You are coming home with us, and that is that."

"I—" John said.

"No more arguments," Mac said. He called for the check.

"John, I promise you," Rachel said, "we're going to get you on your feet and straighten out your life, even if I have to take on your wife and Steve Frame to do it!"

Chapter Eleven
Too Much and Not Enough

In the two weeks following Lenore's day off, she noticed a distinct change in Robert. And at first, she thought it was good.

Guilt-ridden over the bad turn her marriage had taken, Lenore decided she was mostly to blame. Yes, Robert was dead set against her career at Frame and yes, she didn't agree with Robert's philosophy of wife-at-home, but she felt she could handle things much better. Maybe if she went out of her way to give him some of the things he wanted, he would respond by compromising on her career aspirations.

So Lenore set her plan in motion. She rose half an hour earlier to prepare Robert the breakfasts he loved. She left work fifteen minutes early to rush home and whip up dinners that dazzled the eye as well as the palate. She kept herself beautiful, sexy and giving. In conversation, she avoided any areas of controversy.

Robert, Lenore thought, was responding well. Gone were his petty little demands, his nagging criticisms and his various complaints. Though he was not overly affectionate, Lenore thought she was off to a good start.

But after a week of this, Lenore slowly began to realize that something had changed. She knew that Robert was not responding because of what she was trying to do to please him. Robert had grown apathetic. He didn't really notice or care about the extra effort she was attempting to put into their marriage. He didn't call her from the office anymore, or ask what was for dinner, or ask how Wally was doing. More and more, he remained very late at work and would sometimes fall asleep at the office and not come home until two or three in the morning.

Lenore wanted to confront him with this, but she was frightened and confused. It seemed to her that her new plan to please him had backfired and alienated him. Couldn't she do anything right?

At wit's end, she called Janet into her office, closed the door and asked Janet what she thought.

"Maybe he's having a mid-life crisis," Janet said. "Men go through that."

"That can't be it," Lenore said.

"Then he's having problems at work. You know how that can be—ecstatic one day, then depressed and doubtful the next."

"His business is booming, better than ever."

Janet shook her head. "It's hard to understand men sometimes. Just when you think they're angels, they stick you with a pitchfork. There might be another reason, though."

"What?"

"It's kind of hard to say," Janet said. "And it's only a wild guess, but you don't think Robert is seeing another woman, do you?"

"Absolutely not!" Lenore said. "He's moody, yes, and I guess I haven't been the perfect wife, but I trust him, Janet. He was single for a long time before he met me, and he could have had any number of women. He knew what he was doing when he married me, he knows what marriage is about. No, he's committed, I'd bet on it."

"Good," Janet said. "Good, that makes things a bit easier. Narrows down the possibilities."

After Janet had left, Lenore didn't feel that the conversation had gotten anywhere. She threw herself into her work.

Just before lunchtime, Lenore's phone rang.

"Lenore Delaney," she said.

"You might not remember me," the woman's smooth voice said, "but I met you at your wedding. Carol Lamonte. I work with your husband."

Lenore remembered her only too well. "Yes, how are you?" What on earth could she want? Lenore wondered.

"I'll be brief," Carol said. "I'm worried about Robert."

"What do you mean?"

"I really don't want to talk about it over the phone. Would you mind meeting me? Tonight? At the Cat's Eye Lounge after work?"

Lenore's mind was racing. A golden ray of relief entered her heart. Maybe Robert *was* having problems she wasn't aware of. Maybe, maybe, maybe. "Yes," she said, "I'll be there."

"Terrific. I'll see you then. Bye, now." And Carol hung up.

Lenore sat and thought for many long moments.

Carol didn't strike her as the kind of woman to be so generous, to call up a perfect stranger and offer help. That meant that whatever Robert's problem might be, it was serious. Serious enough for Miss Snippity to approach her.

Lenore couldn't sort out her feelings; she didn't know what to think about any of this. She didn't know if she could trust Carol or not. Was Carol scheming, trying to use Lenore to, perhaps, get ahead in Robert's firm? Or was she really going to tell Lenore of some secret problem that Robert had, which only Lenore could cure?

Doubts, a million doubts.

Then, suddenly, her conversation with Janet came into her mind. Was Robert having an affair—with Carol? The idea was crazy, the stuff of bad movies. But everything that Lenore had ever read or heard about men having affairs always started off with the man ignoring his home life, slipping into silence.

But if that was true, if Robert was having an affair with Carol, why on earth would she call her? What could she possibly want?

Stop it! Lenore screamed at herself. *You're torturing yourself. Your imagination is getting out of control. You're paranoid, you can't handle your marriage and you're an emotional wreck. Take things as they come, and just go see what the heck Carol wants and get it over with.*

Carol, with her hand still on the phone, smiled. Her days of research, of pouring through old newspapers, of asking discreet questions, of generally finding out all she could about Lenore, had led to this one phone call and would lead to bringing Robert permanently into her arms. For men like Robert you had to fight any way you could, and Lenore was no match for Carol Lamonte.

She rose and walked straight into Robert's office. Robert looked up.

"Close the door," he said.

"Something wrong, darling?" she said.

"I feel like dirt," he said. "I'll be honest with you. Our times together are terrific, and I fully admit I've never experienced anything like them. But guilt is tearing me apart and I don't know how much longer I can stand it. Lenore is a fine, caring woman and this would totally destroy her."

"I want to hug away your worries," Carol said, "but since we're in the office I can only promise to do it later. Don't you worry, Bob, what Lenore doesn't know can't hurt her. People make mistakes, and you made one. You fell in love with a woman who can't handle you, your desires, your needs, what you want out of life. Relax, let things happen. Aren't you glad that I'm here for you?"

Robert nodded. "Yes, yes, I am. You know I am. But, I don't know, I feel like I should be trying much more to make my marriage work. Lenore is trying so hard that it tears my heart out. You have no idea what I'm going through."

"I do, believe me," Carol said. "But you can't beat a dead horse, Robert. No need in torturing yourself just because your wife is mixed up and can't handle her own life or you. Leave her be for a while, maybe she'll come around. Give her time to sort things out and come to you with her answer. In the meantime, you won't be lacking for love, and that is a promise I can keep."

Robert started to speak but didn't. He watched

Carol leave his office, wondering what the future held in store.

The Cat's Eye Lounge had a scandalous reputation. A red velvet, small, dark and plush bar and lounge, it was a place where rumors were born, where gossip gushed on a tide of high society scandal. It was a safe haven for men entertaining women who were not their wives, for wives entertaining transient men, and there was plenty of room under the table for political bribes to pass back and forth.

It was there that Lenore had been sitting for the past half hour, nervously sipping her Virgin Mary, too anxious to speculate what the whispering people around her were talking about. But, she admitted, it was the perfect setting for a clandestine meeting with your husband's mistress. For that is what Lenore had finally decided. And if Carol was not Robert's mistress, then only good news and great relief awaited her. Better to guess the worst and be wrong than to hope for the best and be slapped in the face.

When Carol appeared in the entranceway, Lenore didn't at first recognize her. She didn't remember Carol as being this stunning, this sultry, this, let's face it, sexy. Bright-blond hair, sparkling eyes and a figure that stretched the peach dress Carol was wearing —*this is the competition?* Lenore asked herself. How could she possibly win?

Lenore waved discreetly, then stood. Carol approached with a large smile.

"Hello, Lenore, thanks for coming," Carol said. "It's good to see you again."

"You, too," Lenore said. So cool, so in control, she thought defensively.

A tall hostess in a short black skirt and a white satin blouse with huge shoulders approached Carol. "May I get you something from the bar?"

"Yes," Carol said. "Scotch, straight up." The hostess left. Carol said to Lenore, "It's been a hard day."

"Mine, too," Lenore said. What else could she say? Carol had called her here, and Lenore was dying of curiosity and tension. Still, she kept silent until Carol's drink arrived.

Meanwhile, Carol was sizing up Lenore. *A tad mousy, she thought, but pretty. Very pretty, in fact. She's nervous, though, and she shows it. An emotional type, definitely. And as I well know, she's had the kind of life to be emotional about.*

Carol had her little scheme all worked out. And surprise was the key to her plan for success.

"I'll be frank with you, Lenore," Carol said.

Lenore shifted in her seat. "Please do."

"Robert's got a problem and he came to me. So I know quite a bit about you. In fact, I know a lot."

"Sorry," Lenore said, "I don't know what Robert's problem has to do with your knowing about me."

"I'll explain," she said. "It's no secret around our office that you and Robert are having, shall we say, troubles. Robert and I have been close for a while, so, naturally, he confided in me. He said you were married before to a man named Walter, and you were afraid of marriage because of what happened to your first relationship."

Lenore's heart started beating furiously. *Don't panic*, she thought. *Don't be intimidated. Say something, for crying out loud.*

"Miss Lamonte," Lenore began, "my past history is

really none of your concern, no matter what Robert confided. Actually, our marital problems are none of your business, either. Robert and I can surely handle those ourselves."

Carol laughed. "I'm sure you can. But, you see, your problems have involved me, too."

Lenore, extremely upset now, blurted, "I know you've been seeing Robert."

Carol's big green eyes widened. "Oh, you do? Well, I wonder where you heard that nasty bit of gossip. Don't believe everything you hear, Lenore. Just because you and Robert are having troubles, there's no need to get paranoid."

This woman is vicious, Lenore thought. She also knew she was no match for her, no matter what her little game was.

Lenore grasped her purse. "I don't have to sit here and listen to this."

"You should hear one more thing," Carol said firmly. "I know about Walter. All about him."

Lenore inhaled sharply. Could Carol mean what she thought she meant? *It isn't possible,* thought Lenore. *I'm the only person on earth who knows the truth about Walter, that Walter was a murderer. Aren't I? Yes, of course, I am. Minutes after Walter confessed to me, he was killed in a car accident. He'd called no one, spoken to no one. Carol has to be bluffing. God, please, she has to be bluffing.*

"Everyone knows about Walter and me," Lenore said. "The terrible car accident was in all the papers."

"But I'll just bet," Carol said, "that there's something that didn't make the papers. Something you surely wouldn't want the world to know. Something you wouldn't want Robert to know."

"You're threatening me," Lenore said. "You're trying to pull something here, and you don't know what you're talking about. What do you want? Why are you doing this?"

Carol stood and smoothed down her dress. "I'll just let you think about it for a while. Call me anytime." And Carol turned and left the Cat's Eye Lounge.

On the way out, Carol's knowing smirk fell into a frown. She had, of course, been bluffing, trying to scare Lenore, perhaps touch a raw nerve. And somehow Lenore had learned about her affair with Robert. It hadn't worked out as she'd planned, not at all. Carol hoped she hadn't made a huge mistake.

Lenore was shaking. She couldn't think about standing. She had to rest, catch her breath.

Suddenly it didn't matter at all whether or not Carol was sleeping with Robert, although Lenore was certain she was. What mattered now, more than anything in the world, was Wally. If Wally ever found out that his father had been a murderer, Lenore knew it would ruin the boy for life. She loved Wally more than anything in the world, and she had to protect him from this one horrible fact; it was the only lie she would ever tell him.

Did Carol know? There were ways to find out anything if you really wanted to know. Ultimately, Lenore decided, it didn't matter. She couldn't take the risk.

"Is anything wrong?" asked the hostess.

"What?" Lenore said, startled. It was then that she discovered she had been crying. "Oh, no. Just some bad news, that's all. Thank you."

"Let me know if I can get you anything," she said.

"No, thank you."

The hostess left.

Lenore rose and hurried into the women's room, locked herself in a stall and began crying heavily. This one dark cloud in her life had again moved overhead. There would be no reconciliation with Robert. There would be no more arguments about breakfasts, her career, her duties as a wife. No longer would she have to twist her life inside out trying to please him, trying to understand him.

Her life with Wally had to, and always would, come first. She had to protect him at all costs.

The tragedy of it all brought on a new wave of deep sobs.

The following morning, Lenore gave her notice at Frame Enterprises. She'd be leaving in two weeks.

During those weeks, she knew she had to confront Robert and tell him her plans. It would hurt him deeply, but she could not afford to give him much of an explanation.

More importantly, she had to have a long talk with Wally. She had to come up with some way to explain to the innocent boy why his mother was suddenly packing their bags, leaving house, home and husband and taking them far away from Bay City forever.

Chapter Twelve
Hoping and Healing

There was the promise of winter in the wind: it held a chill that brought scarves and sweaters out of the closet. It reminded people of the passage of time. It was the wind of change.

For Rachel and Mac, the last couple of weeks had not been easy. It was the strength of their marriage and caring that saw them through this tough time. For John, residing in their home, struggling to free himself of demons he'd lived with for many months, needed constant emotional support.

It took only a couple of days for Rachel to realize that her plan of resurrecting John's life was too idealistic. The second day in their home, he simply vanished in the late afternoon and did not return. Rachel found him, at three in the morning, at a seedy bar on the outskirts of town. He had cried then, pleading weakness, saying it was too late to help him. She refused to listen to failure. She grabbed him by the collar and dragged him home. Rachel knew that she and Mac needed help with him. But from whom, they weren't yet sure.

Mac took John out on the town to the best men's shops and purchased a few suits, cleanly tailored, dark-blue pin-striped and dark brown. New shoes, a haircut. Through it all, John was sheepish. He protested mildly, weakly, shaking his head many times and saying he couldn't see how this would work.

"Clothes don't make the man," John said. "I appreciate it, but inside—well, I guess I'm a coward."

Mac got tough.

"You're absolutely right, John," Mac said. "Clothes certainly do not make the man. Know what makes the man? Spirit. Spunk. Confidence. Come on, John, we're going to my club. A few sweaty sets of handball will do you a world of good."

"Or give me a heart attack," John protested.

Neither man had a heart attack. They played hard and they played well. John tired early but he kept with it, and Mac noticed a determination in John's eyes he had not seen before. Yes, the spirit of competition was very healthy, indeed.

Two days ago, Mac and Rachel had felt that John was nearly all the way there. So Rachel sat him down and explained her plan, in part.

"John, we're proud of you," she said.

John smiled. "It's this old coot here. Did he tell you that I finally beat him at handball today? Whew, what a game! Yessir, I feel like a new man, thanks to you two."

Rachel was proud of herself, too. "But, John," she said, "this is only the beginning."

"What do you mean?" John said. "I'm off the booze, I'm in pretty decent shape. I was kind of thinking about leaving in a day or so."

"And you will," Rachel said. "But first you've got to get your life in order. Your career, and the rest."

John's face darkened. "I've been avoiding thinking about that. Frankly, I'm at a loss as what to do. Sure, I could open a law office again, but who'd come to me? My reputation is still garbage."

Mac looked at Rachel and she nodded. Mac smiled.

"What's going on here?" John said, noticing the exchange.

"I made a phone call today," Rachel said, "to your wife, Pat. We had a nice talk. She'll be expecting you for dinner on Saturday."

John was shocked. He also didn't know how he felt about seeing Pat again. Yes, he still loved her, loved her dearly. But, in a way, he blamed her for starting his drinking and decline. She, like the rest of the town, thought he was a Judas for sending Steve Frame to prison. And having the woman you love turn against you like that was more than any man could take.

So, did he want to see her? Yes, he did. Could he ever forgive her for not sticking by him? Of course he could.

"What'd you say to her?" John said. "I mean, why am I going over there?"

"She's willing to talk," Rachel said. "I told her you'd made a remarkable recovery. She still loves you, John. But you two have some peace to make, and she's willing to take the first step."

Rachel was stunned to see a transformation take over John. It was as though a dark cloud of doubt moved over his face, drawing down his expression, glazing his eyes, slumping his shoulders.

"I hope I can handle it," John said.

"If you can trounce me in handball," Mac said loudly, "you can do anything!"

John smiled weakly but said no more.

That Saturday morning, John came downstairs, paused to ruff Jamie's hair and tease the dog, then went into the breakfast room, where Mac and Rachel were eating grapefruit.

"Good morning," Mac said. "Breakfast?"

"No, thanks," John said.

"Hi, John," Rachel said.

"Morning," John said. "Tonight's the night, huh?"

Rachel lowered her spoon. "Yes, it is. What's the matter?"

John shrugged. "I guess I'm nervous. I feel like I'm going to propose to her, you know? In a way, I am. I'll be going in there asking to come back into her life. But what do I have to offer her? What's a man who has no work, who's lost his career?"

"Stop that," Mac said. "You're a great guy and a great human being. You're you, and you're worth loving. You've gone through hell and you've survived. What more do you think she wants?"

John shrugged again.

Rachel began to grow fearful. She knew he was slipping away, indulging himself in his insecurities, a habit he'd created over the past few months. If he only knew how much he needed Pat, what a world of good she could do for him.

"I think," John said, "I'll just go out for a walk. Be alone, you know? Do some thinking."

Mac and Rachel looked at him.

"Don't worry, I'll stay away from the bars," John said, looking at the floor. "I'll be back soon, you'll see."

John turned and walked out of the house.

"I smell trouble," Mac said.

"Poor John," Rachel said. "He's lost his dignity."

"Want me to go fetch him back?" Mac asked.

"No, hon. Let him be. He's got to work this out for himself."

Mac swallowed a spoonful of grapefruit. "You know, I wish I could give him a job, get him back in the work force again, doing something productive."

Rachel shook her head. "I think his problem's deeper than that. I don't think he really wants a new life. I think he wants his old one back."

Mac chuckled. "Well, that's an impossible dream."

Rachel suddenly sat upright. "Is it? Is it really?"

Mac clapped his hands. "You've got another idea?"

"Yes," Rachel said. She wiped her mouth and stood. "When I mentioned it before, I was really just trying to cheer up John. Oh, why didn't I do it before?"

"Do what?"

"I'm going right over and have a talk with the one man who can put the fire back in John's life. I'm going to see Steve Frame."

Mac's excited look vanished. He frowned.

Rachel went to him, took his face in her hands and planted a kiss on his puckered lips. "Oh, don't look so worried, you big baby. I'm all grown-up now. I'm going to talk to him adult to adult. If it works, it works. If it doesn't, it doesn't. I won't be long."

"Maybe I should go with you," Mac said.

"Great! Come on, let's go!"

Mac shook his head. "Naw. I see what you mean. I guess you've got something to settle with Steve, too."

"I love you, Mackenzie Cory. Bye!"

* * *

Rachel returned two hours later. She knew Mac must have been watching for her, because he opened the door before she even reached it.

"How'd it go?" Mac said.

"Well," Rachel huffed, "not too badly. Talking to him was easier than I thought. I'm not sure whether he forgives me for the past or not, but I do know that he and Alice are happy. It shows in his face, in his manner, and made him a lot more confident."

"What about John? Did you talk about John?"

"I did," Rachel said. "I tried to explain things from John's point of view. I told him about John's recovery, and everything. He said he'd think about it."

"That's all he said?" Mac said. "And you settled for that answer?"

"I had no choice, Mac."

"I knew I should have gone with you. Used a little of my negotiating genius on him. Twisted him around my little pinky until he begged for John to come back to work for him."

Rachel patted Mac on the cheek. "I know, I know."

"Well, I would've," Mac said.

"Is John home?"

"No."

Rachel's heart flipped. "What? He really hasn't come back?"

"Nope, and I'm worried," Mac said. "I was thinking about calling the bars around town, but thought I'd wait for you."

"Let's not," Rachel said. "John has to find himself. I wonder where he is?"

During the next hour, Rachel asked that question

another ten or twenty times. Then, for the next two hours, she had to nearly physically restrain Mac from going out to look for John.

"We're due at Pat's house in an hour," Mac said.

"I know, I know," Rachel said.

"So, what are we going to do? Call her? Tell her the whole thing's off?"

"Not yet. Please. Come on, let's go up and change. That'll keep our minds off it."

Forty minutes later, they were dressed and downstairs.

"I'm calling Pat right now," Mac said. "We'll look like fools, and it'll probably break her heart, but it's better than not calling at all or going over there empty-handed."

Rachel was near tears. "All right. Call her."

At that moment, the doorbell rang.

Mac walked to the door and opened it.

"John!" Rachel said.

John stood there smiling. "Worried about me?" he said.

Mac immediately leaned forward and sniffed John's lips. "If you've been drinking," Mac said, "you've been doing it through your ears."

John entered. He was holding a large arrangement of flowers. "Got some flowers for Pat."

"John, we were so worried," Rachel said. "Where were you?"

"Sitting and thinking, mostly," John said. "Took a walk. I ended up in the library. Then I fell asleep. I woke up about an hour ago. Am I late?"

"You've got just about three minutes to get changed and get out of here," Mac said. "Gimme those flowers, and move it!"

174

John headed toward the stairs and stopped. He walked over to Rachel and kissed her cheek. "Thank you for all you've done. You, too, Mac. I think it was worth it. I think I'm ready to get back to being me. Why, if it weren't for you two, I'd still be—"

Mac cut him off. "Will you shut up and get changed? You can embarrass us in the car."

John laughed and hurried upstairs.

Pat Randolph didn't have particularly high hopes. She had watched her husband rise to become one of the most prestigious corporate lawyers in the state. And, more recently, she had watched John deteriorate. She might have been able to forgive John for betraying Steve Frame, but it was harder to forgive John for what he'd eventually done to himself. And when John's drinking had begun to ruin not only his own life but their marriage and good name as well, she couldn't live with him anymore. The sight of her drunken husband walking out the door was a memory permanently etched in her mind—and her heart.

Now, as she moved along the dining-room table, double-checking the place settings and reminding the cook and the attendants about this and that, she shook her head. Who would have believed, even a short year ago, that Rachel would turn into a human being? And it was Pat's ability to totally forgive and actually like Rachel that led her to believe that possibly she could also forgive her husband. But could Rachel work the same miracle on John as she had on herself? It remained to be seen.

She checked the grandfather clock. They'd be here any minute. She walked to the mirror beside the large, sweeping staircase and looked into her own blue eyes, studying her pleasingly round face and short-cropped hair. Pat liked a style that bordered on the severe, but tonight she opted for a softer look, rosier rouge, a simple string of pearls, a cream-colored cotton dress. For some reason that escaped her, she felt young tonight.

The doorbell rang, and there was John, holding a large bunch of fresh flowers.

Mac and Rachel stood behind John, saying nothing, watching the silent drama unfold.

John smiled, a sparkle in his eye, the old sparkle. Pat returned his smile. It would be all right, she knew that immediately. John was well again—yes, he was. Tears soon flooded her cheeks, and she and John stepped forward into each other's arms.

After dinner, as they all sat in the expansive living room decorated with turn-of-the-century furniture, the atmosphere was relaxed and tension free.

"Will you stop apologizing?" Pat said to John. "Once was enough, and now it's getting embarrassing."

"Sorry," John said. "I did it again, didn't I?"

Rachel checked her watch for the fifth time in half an hour.

"Pat," Mac said, "you've got to understand men. When they lose their pride, like John did here, strange things happen to them. A man thinks pride is just about all he is, and when he loses it he feels like he's no good to anyone, particularly himself. But then, when he gets his pride back, he feels as though he'd done something wrong, like it was all his fault that he's human. You know what I'm trying to say?"

Pat smiled. "No." All laughed. "All I know is that John and I are both grateful for friends like you. And

Rachel, I just have to ask you right out, what happened to you? Did Mac cast some kind of spell on you?"

Rachel blushed. "I guess he did, Pat."

The phone rang. Soon the butler entered the room. "Telephone for Mr. Randolph."

"Me?" John said, rising. "Wonder who that could be?"

Rachel crossed her fingers and glanced at Mac. Mac winked and crossed his fingers, too.

Pat caught all of this but said nothing.

Ten minutes later, John came slowly back into the room. He was scratching his head and smiling like sunshine.

"John?" Pat said.

"You're not going to believe this," John said. "You are just not going to believe this. Do you know who that was? Do you?"

"Not until you tell us," Pat said. "Who?"

"That, my dear wife, was none other than Mr. Steven Frame himself."

"Steve Frame!" Pat said.

John held his arms wide. "He wants me back! He said he wants to forgive and forget. And then he *asked* me if I would consider being Frame Enterprises' counsel again. I can hardly believe it!"

"And what did you say?" Rachel asked.

"What do you think I said? I said yes."

"Why on earth did he call?" Pat asked. "What made him call you, what changed his mind about you?"

"He said he'd been giving the whole thing a lot of thought," John said. "He said he just couldn't lose one of his best friends because I was only doing my job. He admitted he'd done wrong and he said he'd be a real coward not to admit it. But most of all, he said he would never have had the courage to call me if it weren't for one person: Rachel."

"Rachel?" Pat said, looking at Rachel. "You convinced Steve Frame to hire John back? You, the woman—I'm sorry, Mac—the woman who nearly ruined his life? How'd you do it?"

Rachel waved her hand in the air. "Oh, I think he was ready for it. He felt guilty over John. He knew that John was only being the honest man he's always been. I really didn't have to say much."

"But you said something," John said. "What on earth did you say?"

"People change," Rachel said. "All I did was to start the conversation off with two very important words: 'I'm sorry.'"

Steve Frame hung up the phone in the study of his mansion. Alice was sitting on the leather sofa and he joined her. She handed him a glass of lemonade, and he sipped it and smiled.

"I feel like a million," Steve said, slipping his arm around her.

"I'm proud of you," Alice said. "I'm proud of Rachel, too. And John. You know, it's like the entire town is healing itself."

Steve nodded. "I know what you mean. How could I have been so stupid? John's an honest man, and I wasn't. He got me sent to prison, but I deserved it. I need an honest man around me and, believe me, honest men are hard to find in my business. Having someone close at hand whom you trust is very rare."

"And having a big heart like yours is rare, too," Alice said, kissing his cheek.

"My heart is a slow learner," Steve said. "But now, things will be just fine." He took another sip. "I still find it hard to believe how much Rachel has changed."

"She really has."

"I mean, she's actually a nice person, a *real* person. It's a darn miracle."

"And she's pretty, too," Alice said.

"Always has been," Steve said. "And—hold it. Are you getting jealous?"

"Who, me?"

"You are. You're jealous. Alice is jealous."

"No, I'm not. Don't be silly."

Steve put down his drink and surrounded her with his arms. "I'm not the silly one, you are. I love you, more than anyone I've ever loved before. Rachel's reform, her marriage to Mac, John's life back in order and my wonderful life with you are one big happy ending to years of scandal and heartbreak. The world is right again, and I'm going to make the most of it with you."

"Well," Alice said playfully, "I guess I believe you. But you still haven't kissed me."

Steve chuckled, bent her backward on the sofa and kissed her deeply and passionately.

Chapter Thirteen
Good-byes and Good Wishes

The announcement cut through the echoing chatter and bustle of the airport's main waiting area. "Flight 495 now boarding at gate fifteen."

"That's us," Lenore said to Wally.

"I'm scared," Wally said. "I don't wanna fly way up in the sky."

"It's safe, believe me," Lenore said. "You'll love it, Wally. You get to look down *on top of* the clouds."

"On top?" Wally said. "Really?"

"You bet. Come on, honey, we'd better hurry."

It was the afternoon of October fifteenth. The last weeks in Bay City had been the hardest of Lenore's life. But now, silver wings would take her away from all of it, far away to a new life, a new start.

Soon Lenore and Wally were settled in and buckled up.

"What do we do now, Mommy?" Wally asked.

"We wait for the plane to take off. Look out the window there. See the men loading our suitcases into the plane?"

"Wow. What else do we do?"

"Well, we get to see a movie."

"We do?" Wally was excited. "When? What movie?"

"After we take off, we'll get a snack and they'll turn off the lights and show a movie. I don't know which movie yet."

"This is going to be fun! I'm gonna see if I can see our suitcases!"

As Wally watched the men below, Lenore leaned back and closed her eyes with an exhausted sigh. She smiled, thinking about the party her co-workers had thrown for her the night before. Everyone had been there, including Steve Frame himself, who slipped her a "thank you" check for a surprisingly large amount of money. Everyone said they'd miss her, but no one asked why she was leaving. Lenore knew that everyone in that room thought they knew why she was leaving, which, though ugly, made it much easier for Lenore to hide the real reason.

What everyone knew at the party was what Lenore herself had discovered one short week following her strange drink with Carol Lamonte. Once more, Janet Williams had played a key role in her life.

"I've got some shocking news, so prepare yourself," Janet had said, slipping into Lenore's office and closing the door.

Lenore had grasped the arms of her desk chair. "What is it?"

"I've been dating one of the hunks who work with Robert. He told me something, and I believe him. So I thought you should know. Here it is. Robert's cheating on you, the dirty creep."

So it was true, Lenore had thought. And what she had felt then, surprisingly, was more relief than hurt. Though the hurt was definitely there.

"I don't think it'd be fair to tell you who he's been seeing," Janet had said. "It doesn't really matter, does it? But if you add up his late nights out, his moodiness, his apathy and all of that: if you add that to this information from Robert's co-worker—well, I think the facts are clear."

"Carol Lamonte," Lenore had said.

"How'd you know?" Janet had said. Surprise had widened her face.

Lenore had shrugged. "An educated guess." Tears had started falling from her large eyes.

"I'm sorry, Lennie," Janet had said. "I really am."

A blond stewardess came around checking their seat belts and asking if they needed anything.

"Hi!" Wally said to her.

Lenore kissed Wally and sat back in her seat.

As things had turned out, she did not have to lie to Robert about her reason for leaving. His unfaithfulness gave her all the reason she needed, and all the reason Robert had to know. When she had confronted Robert with his affair, he had freely admitted it, cried and apologized, but Lenore had told him it was over. That evening, she had moved out into a hotel room, filed for divorce and begun making plans to leave Bay City. Also that evening, she had taken her frightened and confused son aside and tried to explain things to him.

Again, Lenore was grateful she did not have to tell her son a lie.

"But, Mommy, I don't want to leave," Wally had said. "I like it here. I like my friends."

"I know, honey," she'd said. "But sometimes things don't work out the way you want them to. Mommy has a big problem, and I'm very, very sad about it."

"You are?"

"Yes. You see, Bob has found someone else that he loves more than he loves me."

"Why?"

"I don't know, Wally. But we can't live with someone who doesn't love us, can we?"

"I guess not," Wally had said. "But why can't we just move down the street?"

"Well, that's hard to explain. But if we did move down the street, I'd still see Bob in the town or in a restaurant. And just seeing him would make me sad all over again."

Wally had hugged Lenore. "I love you, Mommy."

"I know you do. And I love you. I'm sorry you're sad, too. But things will be better real soon. You'll see. Just you and me, we're going to find a new house, new friends, and have the best time we've ever had in our lives."

Lenore was proud of Wally. He took the entire thing bravely, and she felt that he even understood a bit of what she felt.

Yes, she firmly believed that things would be better. This was a time for celebration, not for tears. It could have been much worse, but Robert's adultery solved a very ugly situation quickly. She had loved and lost, but she had learned. And she would grow.

With a gleeful shriek from Wally, the plane lifted him and Lenore off the fertile earth of Bay City. As the skyline disappeared from view behind a wisp of cloud, so did all connections with her painful past. At last she was free, flying into the sun and a brighter future.

Robert knew he had made the biggest mistake of his life. He was a victim, and he wasn't quite sure how it all had happened. But it had, and it tore out his soul.

Now, instead of having a warm home after work, he warmed the bar stools around town, drowning in self-pity, regret and anger.

He knew someday he'd bounce back, get ahold of the life he had had before he'd met Lenore. But for now, he couldn't stand being in his own empty home. He couldn't be alone with his questions, with his failures. He needed the company of people who understood, who gathered in the gin mills to silently acknowledge each other's pain by their mere presence.

"Another," Robert said to the bartender. Then he laughed at himself. He had thought himself to be invincible, king of the hill, a self-made millionaire with the world at his feet, with life there for the taking. He had never expected that his heart could break.

He hadn't lost in a very long time, and the pain of it all reminded him that he was, indeed, a human being and that there were other things in the world that brought rewards far greater than money or power. There were things to gain in life that success could blind you to.

Yes, he'd soon seek them again. But not for a while.

Carol Lamonte sat at home, staring at the unopened boxes she had mailed to herself from the office. She was trying to tell herself that she didn't care, but her tears defied her.

She had thought she had won. When Lenore had moved out of Robert's house and his life, she thought her scheme had borne the fruits of delicious victory. She fantasized about her and Robert's life together. She'd move into his fantastic house, she'd give him everything he needed. The end justifies the means, she reasoned. Now Robert was with a real woman, a woman who'd fought for him and deserved him.

Yes, she had thought she had won. But when Robert had called her into his office and abruptly fired her, told her to pack her things and leave immediately, the shock was almost too much to bear.

Robert wouldn't give her a reason. He was cold, hard, bitter. He told her he would not see her again, and couldn't even stand to see her in the office for another minute.

She made the mistake of asking if he'd found out about her meeting with Lenore. She explained that she loved him dearly and was only trying to protect him from his loveless wife. Could he blame her for fighting for him? Could he blame her for helping him out of a horrible marriage? Could he blame her for wanting the best for him?

He blamed her, and blamed her viciously.

Gone, all gone. Yes, she'd successfully driven Lenore out of his life. But she had never expected that Robert's heart would break.

As Lenore and Wally flew into the sky, as Robert sank into his fourth bourbon and as Carol counted the few remaining pieces in her empty life, an odd but joyous reunion was taking place in the grand dining hall of the Bay City Hotel.

Together at a huge, round banquet table was a group of people the press would have bet a year's earnings would never come together for more than five minutes without a gunshot. Yet here they were, decked out in their finery, with flashbulbs popping and a strange mixture of excitement, anticipation and tension in the air.

Pat and John Randolph—she with diamond earrings, a deep-green satin gown, mink draped over her shoulders, he in a wide-lapeled black tuxedo. She was wondering where they might take their spring vacation. He was just overjoyed to be back with the living.

Alice and Steve Frame—she with a stunning diamond necklace, stark-white silk gown, deep sable wrap, he in a sharp dark-blue tux and heavy gold watch and pinky ring. She was marveling at the press, a new experience for her. He was sharing a deeply felt smile with John.

Ada and Gil McGowan—she in a simple formal dress of heavy maroon silk, baby Nancy cradled in one arm, and he in his finest pin-striped vested suit. She was grinning at everyone over every little thing her child did. He, although uncomfortable with such a wealthy crowd, was having fun playing cop in his mind, wondering if anyone had a concealed weapon.

Rachel and Mac Cory—she with an open-necked, full-skirted gown of pale-blue linen, topped off by the emerald necklace Mac had given her on their wedding day, and he in an outlandish navy-blue tuxedo. She somehow felt the center of attention, as if she had done something prestigious. He was wondering why Gil McGowan was staring at everyone's jackets and purses.

And Iris Carrington, wearing a slinky blood-red gown that plunged to her waist in the back, stunning fox wrap, elbow-length white gloves. She was wondering why in the world she had come.

All looking their best, they were a showcase of some of Bay City's elite, a gathering of people whose combined pasts filled the newspaper archives with the juiciest scandals in the town's history.

Pert, attentive waiters and waitresses efficiently

filled champagne glasses and served hors d'oeuvre platters.

The dinner had been arranged by Rachel. Both she and Mac thought it appropriate; indeed, they thought it necessary. Bay City was on the verge of a new era, and all the people sitting around the table this evening were to be the pioneers.

The preliminary conversation, over cocktails, was stilted and awkward. But all knew what they had been through and how things had changed, and the understanding among them was spoken not with words but with smiles, nods and physical presence.

Only Iris Carrington stood out like a sore thumb. Without an escort, without even an ally, she stood apart with a frown on her lovely face, eyeing everyone suspiciously, returning greetings with sarcastic remarks. And being seated next to her father did not improve her appetite or her humor.

After the champagne was poured, Rachel tapped her glass with a knife and stood. Flashbulbs popped and the crowd fell silent.

"Thank you all for coming," Rachel said.

"Hear, hear!" John said.

This drew a mutual giggle.

"I'd like to make a toast," Rachel said, lifting her glass with two fingers.

When Mac stood, so did everyone else. Little Nancy gurgled, and all laughed again.

"I think that kid's had enough," Mac said.

All laughed, and Ada proudly kissed her daughter.

"To us," Rachel said. "To loves and losses. To friends and forgiveness. To new beginnings. And to never looking back. There's more than a future out there for all of us. It's a new future, a future none of us would have thought possible a year ago. But things have changed, we have changed and we have grown. Bless all of you."

They all clinked the crystal glasses and sipped.

All, that is, except Iris. Ever-scheming, she was wondering what Rachel was up to with the dinner. Surely she wanted something, surely there was something behind all this gush. To her, the future held only the promise of victory over her foolish father's impossible wife.

Iris thumped her fingers on the tablecloth, and then was suddenly astounded at the attention that was now riveted on her. A photographer moved in close and shot her. Another flashbulb burst from a distance. All eyes were upon her, and the silence was almost too much to bear.

Mac said, "Oh, you are so stubborn!" Then, suddenly, he uncharacteristically threw a huge arm around Iris's shoulder and planted a kiss on her powdered cheek.

Shocked, stunned, Iris lost her composure. Her eyes flew open, a gloved hand went to her mouth, she blushed furiously and then plopped into her chair.

Hearty laughter rang out. It was just what the other guests needed, the perfect appetizer to the best evening anyone could remember ever enjoying.

Only from Pioneer Communications Network, Inc.

OVER 5 MILLION BOOKS IN PRINT!